SUMMER AT ROSE HALL

Tanya Jean Russell

SAPERE
BOOKS

SUMMER AT ROSE HALL

Published by Sapere Books.

20 Windermere Drive, Leeds, England, LS17 7UZ,
United Kingdom

saperebooks.com

ISBN: 978-1-80055-675-1

CHAPTER ONE

Looking up at the huge manor estate that seemed to spread into the distance, Abby Smith smiled. Her mother, Isabella, might be acting oddly, but it had been longer than she could remember since the pair of them had had a day out together. Plus, this was the first day in months that Isabella hadn't been nagging her about finding a new job.

Walking along the side of the enormous square garden, Abby opened the guidebook she'd purchased at the gatehouse. "They started building Rose Hall in 1594, and apparently it took almost thirty-five years to finish it," she said to her mother, who didn't seem to be listening.

Abby knew that, if she'd been the sort of woman to think about these things, she'd have imagined gliding around the manor in an Elizabethan gown. However, she was far too practical for that. Instead, she cast her eye along the almost weedless lines between the ancient slabs of the paths, and wondered at the amount of workers and organisation it would take to keep a place like this in such perfect condition. She didn't know much about gardening, but even she could see that the flowers blooming in neat squares beside the footpaths were beautifully cared for.

As Abby and Isabella neared the grand house, the late spring sun disappeared behind it. Isabella stopped a few steps behind her daughter and began fiddling with her phone. At the sight of Isabella's eyes darting between the main entrance and the phone in her hand as she lifted her glasses to see the screen better, Abby supressed a smile. She walked back towards her mother.

"Is everything okay?"

"Yes, of course," Isabella replied, a little sharply.

Once the phone was safely back in her handbag, she glanced again at the main entrance to Rose Hall before turning her attention to her daughter. Her gaze drifted over the trouser suit she'd insisted Abby wear today, her frown deepening as she adjusted the collar of the blouse and attempted, yet again, to convince Abby she should undo the top button.

"Mother!" Abby protested, although she quite liked wearing a suit. It reminded her of being on parade back in the army. "I agreed not to wear jeans or combats today, but that's the limit. If I'm wearing this suit, I'm wearing it how I want to."

She might be a civilian now, but that didn't mean the years of strict adherence to the uniform rules were completely gone. It was strange enough wearing a suit without a tie, never mind having her blouse hanging open as well. Not wanting to spoil their day together, Abby resisted the urge to sigh. To be fair, being properly turned out was something that Isabella had tried to instil in both her children for years. It seemed that, despite choosing to marry outside of the titled and wealthy families she'd grown up with — even if it had meant she'd been financially cut off — Isabella hadn't been able to shake off all the training that had come with that life.

Taking a step back and letting her hand fall, she gave an awkward smile before her gaze darted back to the entrance.

"Shall we go in?" Abby asked.

Isabella looked at her, blinking furiously before shaking her head. "Let's enjoy looking at the hall for a moment before we go in."

With a shrug, Abby turned her attention back to the huge building in front of them.

"Dear Isabella!" called a voice so full of elongated vowels that Abby was surprised a single consonant had survived. A tall, slim, tweed-clad woman was walking towards them, three mud-splattered cocker spaniels winding around her ankles. "It has been far too long," the woman added.

"Lady Beaumont," Isabella replied. "How wonderful to see you."

"Oh, none of that nonsense," the woman said, a wide smile on her face. "We're far too old friends to stand on ceremony, besides which, the Beaumont title went long before my time."

"Old habits, Beatrice," Isabella said with a smile, before she gave a nod that Abby felt carried more weight than necessary for a simple introduction. "This is my daughter, Abigail."

Sticking her hand out, Abby shook off the growing sense of unease and smiled at Beatrice Beaumont. Recognising her name, she realised that Beatrice owned Rose Hall. It seemed that Isabella's choice of venue for their day out had been anything but random. Abby didn't know what the plan was, but it was clear something was afoot.

"Why don't you both join me for a spot of tea?" Beatrice suggested.

"That would be lovely, wouldn't it, Abigail?" Isabella said with determination.

"Yes, of course," Abby said, knowing she had no choice but to let things play out.

"We'll go to the estate offices," Beatrice said. "I'd take you up to the family quarters, but I need to clean this rabble before I venture upstairs."

Without waiting for a response, she swept past, leading them up the three large steps and through the main entrance. It was clear that Beatrice's concern for traipsing mud didn't extend to the worn stone of the entrance hall or the long corridor she led them down, ignoring the enquiring glances of the few visitors exploring the house. Eventually, after so many turns that Abby was glad of the sense of direction she'd honed over her years of service, Beatrice pushed open a heavy wooden door and they entered an office.

Gesturing for Abby and Isabella to take a seat on the mismatched chairs positioned around a battered circular table, Beatrice leant over the wide desk that dominated the other side of the room. With windows on both sides, the views of the gardens and tree lines at the back of the estate were extraordinary.

Leaning over to pick up a phone handset, Beatrice stabbed at the buttons. "Can you bring the tea through now?" she ordered.

Any lingering hope that today wasn't some sort of ambush evaporated. Abby turned and fixed her mother with a hard look. Unfortunately, the glare that had kept any number of hardened soldiers in line over the last decade seemed to be entirely ineffective on Isabella.

The three of them passed the time with small talk, interspersed with memories of the older women's school days, while they waited for the tea to arrive. Once it did, Abby was almost prepared to overlook her mother's scheming. An enormous teapot was surrounded by a wobbling stack of three cups, and more pastries than even Abby could manage to eat.

"Abigail," Beatrice said, drawing her attention once they all had a delicate cup and saucer of tea, and Abby had a plate of pastries, "I gather from your mother that you recently left the army and don't have a job yet."

"That's right," Abby said reluctantly, as she finally understood where this whole situation might be headed.

"I'm sure after serving our country, it is challenging to know what the right path is," Beatrice said, showing a level of understanding that surprised Abby, if only because her mother didn't seem to get it.

She nodded, the mouthful of pastry sticking in her throat as she tried to swallow past the tightness that came whenever she thought about what the future might hold.

"I am in a terribly difficult situation," Beatrice said, pausing to sip from her own cup. Every movement she made looked elegant. "My daughter Cordelia lives with her husband in Canada and is due to give birth to my first grandchild this summer."

Abby studied Beatrice, not really following what this had to do with her, but she nodded and smiled. "Congratulations."

"Thank you," Beatrice said, beaming in a way that only grandparents seemed to manage. Abby had seen that look on Isabella's face often enough when her own grandchildren, Abby's nieces, were around. "Anyway," Beatrice continued, "I would like to spend the summer with my daughter, but I am very hands-on with the running of the estate events. I would hand them over to the estate manager, but she already has a full schedule."

Abby nodded again, still trying to puzzle out where this was going.

"When your mother mentioned your situation to me, I realised this presented a marvellous opportunity for us both." Beatrice's smile seemed to grow even broader. "I appreciate this is unlikely to be something you'll want to do forever, but I was hoping that you would consider being our events manager for the summer. I would then be free to go to Canada, and you could work here for a few months while you decide what you really want for your future."

Abby turned to her mother, who was steadfastly staring at the row of bright paintings on the wall. The tightness in her throat seemed to intensify. Resisting the urge to fidget, Abby turned back to Beatrice, her hopeful expression making her heart sink. "I've never been an events manager. I've never even planned a party," Abby explained, willing Beatrice to understand that she was most definitely the wrong person for this job.

"But you have led military action, managed a squadron, and generally been very well organised," Beatrice said. "I can't imagine the army would have promoted you to sergeant if that wasn't the case."

Abby shook her head. "Yes, but…" She stumbled over her words. "I don't know the first thing about putting on an event."

"Well, the beauty of this situation is that I have already planned the entire summer calendar," Beatrice said. "Every event is arranged, and the suppliers are lined up, with contracts in place. I simply need someone organised and good at keeping people in line, to ensure everything goes smoothly."

"I'm really not sure," Abby said. She might have been able to command her entire troop, but she had a feeling she was fighting a losing battle here.

"Well, obviously you'd want to know a little more about the role," Beatrice said, her smile shifting into something a little more knowing.

She spent the next few minutes talking through the summer schedule. Words like cinema, costumes, weddings and balls swirled around in Abby's head as she tried to take it all in.

Finally coming to the end of her commentary, Beatrice switched her gaze to Isabella. She then turned back to Abby with a knowing look. "And, of course, the job isn't exactly nine to five, so it comes with an apartment. It has a shared kitchen, but otherwise it's private enough. If you were to take the job, it would be sensible for you to live in."

Abby's parents were wonderful, caring people, but the prospect of escaping from under their roof was too enticing to pass up. Abby might not know what her future held, but she knew exactly how she was going to be spending her summer.

CHAPTER TWO

"When will you be able to introduce us to Lord Cheshire?" the man asked, tapping his pen against the signature section of the contract.

Keeping his charming Beaumont smile in place, Quinn studied the man opposite him and attempted to ignore the swooping sensation in his stomach. He'd graduated with a first in business, but after discovering none of the big firms wanted a graduate who might have to leave to take over the family firm at any time, he had been repeatedly reminded that his only value was in his contacts.

"As soon as he's back from his Asia trip," his colleague Charlie said, breaking the silence that Quinn knew he should have filled himself.

"And when will that be?" the man asked, his gaze moving pointedly to the contract he was trying to appear reluctant to sign.

"Just a couple of weeks," Charlie said.

The man pulled the cap from his pen and placed the tip against the paper, before turning his gaze back to Quinn. "Two weeks," he said firmly.

Quinn nodded, his self-respect shrinking even more as he did so. He'd been playing this game for over a decade — shouldn't he have gotten used to it by now?

The man stared at him for a beat longer before finally nodding and signing the paperwork. Then, with a broad smile he stood, indicating that Charlie and Quinn should do the same. "I have another meeting to get to, but thank you for your time, gentlemen," he said, indicating his door with his arm. "Please ensure you contact my secretary with the details of my meeting with Lord Cheshire within the next fourteen days."

"Thank you," Charlie said, stepping back into the expansive reception area.

As Quinn made to follow, the man cleared his throat, pulling Quinn's gaze to his own.

"I'd hate to have to use the cooling-off clause in this contract," he said quietly, making the reason for his interest in working with Charlie's business entirely clear.

Holding himself with the confidence that his parents had instilled in him, even if he didn't feel like that person anymore, Quinn gave a sharp nod and followed Charlie.

"I can't believe it," Charlie said, his words tumbling out with excitement. "That's the biggest contract we've secured to date."

The churn of disgust at himself hadn't faded yet, and Quinn found he couldn't share his friend's enthusiasm. He'd met Charlie at university, and after years of working in the recruitment industry, Charlie had decided to set up on his own, offering high-end, exclusive services to the big financial institutions. He'd asked Quinn to join him in a consultancy role, using Quinn's network to open doors that would otherwise have stayed closed to a new business.

Quinn didn't have any qualms about helping Charlie establish his business. He'd been the hardest working person in their circle of friends back at university, and his work ethic had only intensified over the years. If anyone deserved a helping hand to establish themselves, it was him. Besides which, Quinn had done the same for less worthy people in the past.

Unfortunately, years of being valued according to the contacts he had wasn't sitting very well these days.

"Let's celebrate," Quinn said, running his hands through his hair as the image of their avaricious new client swam around his brain. A decent quantity of champagne was the only sure-fire way of shaking off this oily feeling.

"It's only eleven-thirty," Charlie said.

"It's not every day you seal the deal on such a big contract," Quinn countered, desperate to push back his dark thoughts.

"You're right," Charlie said. "Come on, then."

At the bar they frequented, Quinn soon lost track of time. Charlie left sometime between Quinn ordering the third round of drinks, and the rest of the gang turning up. He wondered if he should follow Charlie's example and go home before it became so late that tomorrow was going to be a complete waste. The thought was so fleeting, though, that the sight of Jacinda waving the waiter over to order more drinks sent it flying back out of his mind.

Instead of letting his thoughts linger on how he could add more meaning to his life, Quinn occupied himself with getting smashed. Until Charlie had another target in mind, one that Quinn's impressive surname would be necessary for, he had nothing to do anyway.

Waking the next lunchtime to the sounds of someone clattering around his kitchen, Quinn glanced around. No, he had definitely spent the night alone. Quinn wasn't sure if he was pleased about that or not; he needed to stop the meaningless assignations that simply added to his growing sense of worthlessness, but being alone wasn't particularly appealing either. A few seconds later, the sound of a deep voice singing away let him know that it was just Barney, whose own pad was a little further outside London than was convenient after a night out.

Swinging his legs out of bed and slipping his robe over his pyjama bottoms, Quinn padded out of his bedroom and into the expansive open plan of his apartment.

"Tell me you have at least put the coffee on," he grumbled at his overly cheerful friend.

"Morning, old bean," Barney said.

"What are you doing up so early?"

"Firstly, it's midday, and secondly, I have to get back to the estate today," Barney said.

Quinn resisted the urge to roll his eyes. Only being useful for your contacts was bad enough, but Barney had embraced what Quinn thought was an even less appealing alternative. He was the figurehead for his family estate, a job that was only his by an accident of birth.

"Beatrice has been calling," Barney said.

Quinn's mother was always calling, so he ignored the comment and sank onto his couch, indicating that Barney should pass him a coffee immediately. "How are you finding the job?" Quinn asked.

"It's rather good," Barney said. "We're focusing on equestrian events, so we have a full calendar over the summer, and Kelly is loving it."

Barney had met Kelly at the Olympics the year before. He'd been watching the equestrian jumping, and he'd connected with her at a celebratory event after she'd been awarded the silver medal for individual performance. After a whirlwind romance, they had married in January.

"I suspect she's doing a lot of testing the courses," Quinn said with a laugh.

"She's spending most of her time on the office side of things these days. She's terribly good at the organising," Barney said, his smile making it clear just how besotted he still was with his new wife.

Quinn wasn't at all surprised that Kelly was good at organising. The drive and work ethic it took for her to be so successful in the equestrian field meant she'd excel at anything she turned her hand to. Kelly hadn't grown up on a country estate and didn't come from the sort of monied background many of the top competitors did; she had paid for her riding lessons by mucking out at the local stables and working two part-time jobs.

"How is Kelly finding life as lady of the manor?" Quinn asked.

"Mostly well, but there are still challenging moments," Barney said, his expression suddenly serious. "Daddy's fine, but you know how Mummy is. I catch her wincing occasionally when Kelly speaks. Apparently, she still hasn't got used to the sound of a Yorkshire accent on her Surrey estate."

Quinn sat quietly, wondering just how tough Lady Prestley was making life for her new daughter-in-law.

"Of course," Barney continued, "once Mummy knows that Kelly is going to give her her first grandchild, Kelly's northern roots will be forgiven."

"You're going to be a father?" Quinn asked, leaning forward.

"I am," Barney said, smiling broadly.

"Congratulations!" Quinn said, standing and tugging his friend to his feet so he could pull him in for a bear hug. He didn't quite understand the fascination with babies, but he could see how much this meant to Barney. "I'm delighted for you both. When is the baby due?"

"Not until September," Barney said. "Which means we'll still make it to Miles and India's wedding."

At the mention of the wedding that was being hyped as *the event* of the season by his social circle, rather than the couple themselves, Quinn sat back down. He might get away with avoiding his responsibilities at home for a while, but there would be no avoiding his mother when he went back to Rose Hall for that event. Well, he would have to make the most of the next few months, because he had a terrible feeling that once he returned, he'd be stuck there for good.

CHAPTER THREE

Attempting to ignore Mr Heath, the estate's head housekeeper, Abby started to lift the carefully rolled clothes out of her backpack. The man was tall and so spindly that she wasn't sure how he managed to carry people's luggage. He even had straggly white hair reminiscent of horror movie butlers.

"When are the rest of your belongings arriving?" he asked, his looming presence at odds with his friendly tone. Despite his spooky appearance, Abby could tell that he was making an effort to welcome her.

Glancing at the bed that would be hers for the next few months, Abby quickly supressed her smile before turning back to him. "What do you mean? These are my belongings," she said. For the last few years, she'd gone from one deployment to another, the tours broken up by brief spells at base. It had been easier to have very little by way of physical possessions, and she didn't have much need for anything besides the basics.

"Oh, um, well then, I'll leave you to unpack. Mrs Beaumont will meet you in her office tomorrow morning but has invited you to explore as you wish today," said Mr Heath, backing away awkwardly.

"Thank you," Abby said, giving him a warm smile before continuing to unpack.

She put her underwear and socks in the top drawer of the chest beside the bed, along with her Kindle, chargers and toiletry bag. The scent of lilac wafted out, reminding her of her mum's drawers. Abby took a deep breath; the smell, as far from sand and heat as it was possible to get, seemed to soothe something deep inside. Her pyjamas and casual clothes went into the next drawer, and her more formal wear was placed on hangers in the small wardrobe. With the desk, chair and padded armchair, the room was far more spacious than any bedroom she'd ever had.

Having unpacked, Abby slid her backpack under the bed and went to check out the bathroom. There was a small bath with an overhead electric shower, a spotless sink, and an old-fashioned toilet with its cistern mounted on the wall. She couldn't remember if she'd ever had a bathroom to herself. On deployment, that sort of luxury was only for the most senior of officers. Even back at base, she tended to stay in the single accommodation with its shared facilities.

Leaving her room and walking along the corridor, she peered into the open rooms. They were obviously well cared for, but the battered, mismatched furniture and threadbare carpets distanced the space from the grandeur she'd seen on the floors below. Habit made sure she registered the layout and exit routes, her mind creating a map that she'd be able to follow in the dark. She'd come up the main stairwell, complete with a red velvet rope drawn across a set of enormous double doors that, while not locked, were clearly marked with a 'keep out' sign and had a security camera trained on them. There was also a smaller, back stairway. It had obviously been used by the servants in years gone by, and was still the preferred route for the staff living up here.

As Abby made her way down the back stairwell, she wondered at the kitchen. There was a dated oven and hob, a microwave and a small fridge, but the general piles of detritus made it clear that it wasn't used for much actual cooking. Surely the staff had to be able to feed themselves better than that?

Making her way around the first floor, she clocked the array of exquisitely decorated rooms, all coming from each side of the longest hallway she'd ever seen. The space ran from one side of the expansive building to the other, with windows set in each end. She counted fifteen bedrooms on this floor, on top of the small sitting rooms and other spaces. Abby realised that the Beaumonts couldn't possibly live on this floor because, while richly furnished and decorated, the rooms didn't have any of the touches that would suggest a modern-day family lived in them. Besides which, she wasn't sure anyone would want their bedrooms open to the public. The family must live on the second floor, like her. That surprised her — surely such a wealthy family would normally live in more splendour than that?

On the ground floor, Abby took the time to absorb the space. The entrance hall seemed to be entirely made from stone, almost seamlessly running across the floor and up the walls. The ground floor had fewer rooms, with one side of the building given over to an enormous ballroom with an array of floor-to-ceiling windows. The other side of the ground floor was more of a maze with offices in one corner, which gave way to formal sitting rooms and a beautifully decorated restaurant for what was clearly a very popular afternoon tea.

Almost every table in the restaurant was occupied, the low chatter from each group of diners mingling together. Passing quietly through the restaurant, Abby made her way into the kitchen. It had some mod cons but was still dominated by the sort of features that were reminiscent of the era in which the estate had been completed. A slight woman was directing the activity. No raised voices were needed; simple nods and gestures seemed to keep everything in hand. The white-aproned staff seemed to move around the equipment and each other in an almost balletic way — the kind of cohesion that only seemed to happen when a team had been together for a long time. The thought made Abby swallow hard. She'd had that. She'd chosen to leave, but she missed her team, and sometimes wondered if she'd done the right thing.

"You must be Abby," said the woman who'd been directing everyone, approaching with a smile. "Sorry we can't welcome you properly just now. It's the peak of the afternoon tea service. I'll grab you a plate."

The woman bustled off again before Abby could answer. She wasn't hungry, but she wasn't about to offend the kitchen staff on her first day.

The woman returned. "Here," she said, handing over a plate piled with the most delicious-looking array of miniature cakes and finger sandwiches that Abby had ever seen. "We'll see you before then, but come back here at closing time on Sunday." At Abby's questioning glance, the woman just smiled. "You'll see, but it'll be worth it." She disappeared into the activity surrounding them before Abby could even ask her name.

Slightly bewildered that she hadn't managed to utter a single word in the entire encounter, Abby turned to leave the kitchen. She decided to take advantage of the mild weather, and slipped out of a side door into the garden. Unfortunately, it proved hard to find a quiet spot to enjoy her food. Just as she was about to give up, a hushed voice came from the hedge to her left.

"Hey, you, new girl."

Abby turned. Only her training stopped her from jumping at the sight of a head peering at her from over the hedge.

"Hello," the man said now that he had her attention.

"How do you know I work here?" Abby asked.

"You're on your own, and you have a plate piled high with Donna's best food," he said. "If you're looking for somewhere to hide out, you can squeeze between the wall and the hedge back there."

After a quick glance around, Abby did exactly that. Once through, she found herself in a small space that seemed to have developed by accident, surrounded by mature hedging. The man was waiting for her. Having spent the last decade in the army, Abby recognised the build and strength of someone who had a physical job, rather than someone whose muscles came from the gym. A broad chest filled the deep green polo shirt with the Rose Estate logo on it, letting her know he was another of her new colleagues. A bandage around his forearm and a large plaster on his opposite hand made her wonder just how accident-prone he was.

"So, you planning to share any of that?" he asked, pointing at her food.

"Ah, so the price of your assistance becomes clear," Abby teased. Holding the plate out, she let him help himself.

"Ellis?" a gruff voice called, and her new companion flinched, before taking one more sandwich and stepping back. "Where the devil are you?"

"That's my cue," the man, Ellis, said, giving her a wink. "Better not keep the gaffer waiting."

"Thanks for your help," Abby said as Ellis started to squeeze through the hedges opposite the area she'd entered from.

"I'll definitely see you around," he said, turning his broad shoulders and giving her another wink as he disappeared.

Well, everyone was certainly friendly enough. Abby's mind flickered back to the messages she'd received that morning. The overtly insulting tone of the group chat had made her old team's amusement at her new job abundantly clear. She could only hope that the many disasters they predicted didn't come to pass.

CHAPTER FOUR

Of all the awful ways Quinn could imagine spending his evening, being hijacked by his mother and sister was up there with the worst. Individually they were strong-willed and capable, and he loved them both dearly, but together they were an unstoppable force of nature. He wasn't sure anyone would survive the onslaught of their combined efforts to get what they wanted.

"I said I would think about it," Quinn said, for what felt like the hundredth time. The three of them had been on a video call together for the last twenty minutes.

"I know you have a busy life in London, so I do understand I'm asking a lot," Beatrice said. "And I do appreciate that I'm not giving you very much notice to rearrange things so you can be away."

Quinn knew she was trying to be kind, but they all knew that the life he had here, while generally enjoyable, couldn't be described as busy. It was just that, the minute he said yes to his mother's request, the planning would start, and he'd find himself at the centre of a whirlwind of activity over which he had no control. "I promise I'll think about it," he said again, the words coming out on a sigh as he attempted to ignore the mirrored expressions of the two women he loved most in the world. They always seemed certain that things would happen as they wished, and generally the world bent itself to their will.

"If it helps, Mrs Barclay will be around," Beatrice added.

"It would just be the events, then?" Quinn asked. With his parents' oversight, Mrs Barclay had been running the business side of the estate for years. Her presence would at least give him half a chance of not screwing everything up.

"A lovely woman, Miss Smith, has joined us for the summer, and she will manage the day-to-day running of the events for us," Beatrice explained.

"So, you really don't need me at all then," Quinn said, grasping at an obvious out.

"You know it's important that a member of the family is around. Firstly, there are events that require a Beaumont presence, and secondly, it's our role to co-ordinate everything and be the final decision-maker if different departments can't reach an agreement. I really wouldn't feel able to leave if you weren't here," Beatrice said, picking at some imagined fleck on her blazer as she spoke.

It was a gesture that he knew she used to cover any negative emotion that she felt would be poor manners to let show. A wave of shame washed over him. Great, another opportunity to be a useless figurehead, rather than doing anything useful. Just moments ago, Quinn had been concerned that he was being asked to take on a job he was incapable of doing, so why was he upset to find out that wasn't the case?

"Please think about it, darling," Beatrice said, before making her excuses and saying goodbye.

She always left the group calls first and had once admitted that she liked to give the 'children' — Quinn and his sister Cordelia — a chance to talk without a boring parent around.

"If you say yes, I promise I'll never tell Mother about the time you rode your bike in the long gallery," Cordelia said, waggling her eyebrows.

"You mean the same thing you promised you'd never tell her when you wanted me to do that fête opening so you could disappear to Ibiza for the weekend," Quinn said, wondering what age they'd be when she stopped irritating the snot out of him. "You'll only keep that promise until something else you want crops up."

They both knew their mother wouldn't care that they had both ridden their bikes in the long gallery on a wet and boring day. It was the fact Quinn had wobbled off and broken a vase that had been over two hundred years old that would cause the consternation. As it was, in the face of both her children's determined innocence, Beatrice had seemingly accepted that it was a mystery that would remain unsolved.

"Fine, I won't show her that article with you falling out of a taxi last week," Cordelia said.

Quinn winced. "You won't show her that anyway," he said, on firmer ground here. The siblings both knew that neither would deliberately upset their mother.

"Alright," Cordelia said. "Of course I won't show her. That doesn't mean I'm not worried about you, though."

"It was nothing," Quinn said, his heart sinking. "I'd just had one too many." Unfortunately, he knew he had one too many more frequently than was healthy.

"It was fine when you were younger, but it's starting to feel a lot like you're drowning your sorrows," Cordelia said.

"I'm fine," Quinn said.

"Well, it's not like you have any actual sorrows," Cordelia teased, her tone shifting away from concern.

"I'll think about going home for the summer," Quinn said, surprised to realise that the original conversation was more comfortable than the place they'd drifted to. Glancing around his London apartment, he was acutely aware that even though he paid the bills, the property belonged to Rose Hall. How had he got to this stage in his life and accomplished so little?

"You'll think about it? Come on, Quinn, just do it," Cordelia pleaded.

Quinn realised with a pang that he really missed her. "Just don't add Mother to this call again, please, Cordy," he said, realising he was never really going to refuse, but equally sure he didn't want to deal with his mother and sister when they were both getting their own way.

"You can't avoid making a decision forever," Cordelia replied, her tone more serious as she patted her rounded stomach. "We're on a bit of a time limit here."

"If I do this," Quinn said, "and it's a big *if,* then I will need your help to make sure Mother understands it's a temporary arrangement."

"Nah, you're definitely on your own there," Cordelia said. "It's about time you did something with your life."

The words stung, even though Quinn knew they came from a place of love. "Cheers. We can't all be running our own recycled clothing company by the time we're twenty-eight," he said. He was extremely proud of everything she'd achieved, and continued to achieve, but he wasn't about to make the mistake of telling her that.

"And we can't all be the heir to a massive estate and lands," she said, her expression mischievous as their words echoed a well-worn argument.

"Which you refuse to take!" he said.

"As if I'm daft enough to take that place on. Although, when Father died, I did appreciate your efforts to make it seem like you were doing a favour for the feminist movement by trying to hand the estate over to me. We both know you're only the heir because you're so old."

"I'm only just thirty," Quinn grumbled.

"I know!" she said, with a horrified gasp. "I can't imagine how awful it must be for you. How are your knees holding up? Back giving you trouble?"

"Yes, yes, you're terribly funny and clever. Now, why don't you tell me how Noah is doing? I definitely don't need to hear any more about how you are," Quinn said. He watched Cordelia's eyes light up as she began to talk about her husband.

CHAPTER FIVE

Placing the stack of printed spreadsheets into the drawer and closing it, Abby gave a sigh of satisfaction. The end of her first week had come around quickly, and after spending the first three days with Mrs Beaumont, she had picked up the responsibilities of her new role. Mrs Beaumont was still insisting that Abby call her Beatrice, but despite agreeing to the request Abby still found she couldn't call her that in her thoughts.

Three days in, Mrs Beaumont had given Abby her mobile number and then wandered off with a sea of dogs swirling around her feet, blithely telling anyone who would listen that Abby had everything under control. Mrs Beaumont wasn't particularly well organised, and while a more casual, haphazard approach worked for her, it wasn't going to work for Abby. She was now halfway through producing the expansive wall planner that Mrs Beaumont had agreed she could put up. She was aware that most people didn't use wall planners anymore, instead preferring the convenience of technology, but she liked a visual representation of what was needed. She'd always found that having something her squad could see whenever she was talking to them about their tasks helped them to understand why their duties mattered, and how each individual effort contributed to the success of the unit as a whole.

Abby was hoping it would have the same effect on the team here when it was finished. While she didn't have to deal with any of her own staff in this job, she was entirely reliant on the goodwill and teamwork of the other departments around the estate. They had been friendly and collaborative at the managers' meeting earlier in the week.

Turning, Abby let her gaze wander outside. It was almost seven. The last of the visitors were meandering along the manicured lawn towards the car park. It was lovely seeing couples and friends attempting to eke out the last bit of pleasure they could from the weekend. The warm weather seemed to add to the grandeur. Abby really couldn't be any further from the sand-filled, temporary structures that had served as her home and workplace for the last few years.

The memory turned her thoughts to her old colleagues, her friends, the people she'd left behind, and her throat tightened. Determined not to let herself sink back into that uncertainty, Abby stood. Realising that it was closing time on Sunday, she decided she'd investigate what the chef, Donna, had had in mind when she'd invited Abby to the kitchen.

The sound of laughter greeted her before she stepped through the door. For a brief second, her steps faltered, but she shook off the unfamiliar sense of insecurity and walked in. There were around twelve people gathered, and they were all sipping glasses of bubbly.

"Abby!" Donna said. "Glad you could join us, pour yourself a glass."

Turning to the counter that Donna had gestured to, Abby took in the sight of half a dozen open bottles of champagne. "Are we supposed to…" she started.

Donna laughed warmly. "Don't worry. We get together on Sundays after closing to use up the bottles that we'd be throwing away because they weren't finished. None of them will keep overnight, never mind until we're open again on Wednesday. Sundays are best, as most of this rabble will be off tomorrow."

Taking a glass and filling it, Abby walked over to the gathered group, pleased to realise she recognised all but one of them. Smiling, she raised her glass. "If the rabble gets this sort of treatment, I'm glad to be included," she said.

The responding laughs warmed her, and for the first time in months, Abby felt positive. She hadn't realised just how much she missed being a part of a team. The chatter resumed.

"Did I hear Mrs B say her son was coming back?" Ollie, one of the kitchen staff, asked Donna. "I thought he hadn't been home for years."

"Yes, he is," Donna said. "We're not sure when, but Quinn's coming to help out while Mrs B is away."

There was a snort of laughter at that. Abby turned, realising from the redness of his face that it must have come from Ellis.

"That will do," Donna said, her demeanour changing in an instant. "Quinn is a member of the Beaumont family. He will be head of this estate one day, and we will make sure he knows how welcome he is in his family home."

Looking around, Abby realised that Ellis might have been the only one daft enough to articulate his amusement at the idea of Mr Beaumont overseeing the estate, but there were others who didn't seem entirely pleased by the prospect. If she was honest, though, she would have expected a lot more negativity, given the sort of press coverage the Beaumont heir received. It made her wonder what they were all in for. Well, Abby hadn't led squads for so long without knowing how to get to the bottom of unspoken tensions. She just had to find the right target and the right moment to ask questions, because if there was one thing she hated, it was heading into the unknown.

CHAPTER SIX

Hands clasped behind her back, her posture strong but relaxed, Abby stood in the office. The managers' meeting would be starting shortly, and, without Mrs Beaumont, Abby would be responsible for covering all things event-related. As her new colleagues filtered in, chatting and settling into what were clearly fixed seating arrangements, Abby took the time to observe who chatted with who. Was anyone less involved? Were there any signs of friction?

Glancing once again at the tall clock, she resisted the urge to sigh. The meeting should have started over ten minutes ago. How long did it take people to sit around a meeting table? Taking a deep breath, she straightened her posture even further. Mrs Barclay was running the meeting, but she didn't look like she was planning to get things going anytime soon.

"Should we get started?" Abby asked, her tone brisk and professional.

"We might as well wait for the coffee to arrive," Donna said, the intensity of her gaze belying the casual tone she used.

Abby froze. It had been a long time since one of her *suggestions* hadn't been taken as an order. "The meeting was supposed to start at ten," she said, well aware that some of her irritation was certainly showing now. "It's almost quarter past. I'm sure we all have plenty of work to be getting on with."

"We'll only have to stop to sort out our drinks when everything turns up. It's far less disruptive to wait to start," Mrs Barclay said.

Abby found it hard to believe that a group of experienced managers couldn't pour coffee while continuing with their work discussion. This level of unprofessionalism was alien to her. She'd had plenty of practice getting people to shape up and meet the required standards, but these weren't new recruits. It wasn't down to her to set the standard; she was going to have to get used to the way they did things here instead.

"When are the drinks due to arrive?" Abby asked, wondering if she could make arrangements so that they'd be here before ten o'clock next week.

"Anytime now," Donna said with a shrug, before turning her attention to Mr Heath, who was sitting next to her.

Resigned to a continued delay, Abby sat in the remaining chair and took a deep breath. She wondered how anything ever got done.

As she was mentally reviewing her tasks, the sound of someone mentioning Quinn caught her attention. Abby watched the assembled team from the corner of her eye. Realising it was Mrs Barclay who'd said his name, she focused on her voice.

"At least he'll have grown out of making forts with every spare sheet I have," Mr Heath said indulgently.

"No, instead, he'll have access to every resource the estate has, with no clue how to do anything the estate needs," Mrs Barclay said, the worry in her voice seeming to run deeply.

"He's been busy in London these last few years," Mr Heath said. "I'm sure he's learnt lots of business things."

"We all know what he's been doing in London. Most of the country does," Mrs Barclay said sharply. "And none of it will have prepared him to run Rose Hall, unless the intention is to run it into the ground."

"Rose Hall will be his one day," Mr Heath said, sounding like he was about to fall out with Mrs Barclay.

"I know that, we all do." She sounded weary. "And we care about the boy as much as we do this place. I just hope he'll listen to us."

Mr Heath opened his mouth, but before Abby could satisfy her curiosity about what he was going to say, the door opened and in came the tea and coffee.

The rest of the meeting went well. Despite the way conversation seemed to meander around, they managed to cover the key points, finishing only thirty minutes later than scheduled. It had been a uniquely frustrating experience for Abby. After all, how could she complain when the meeting had achieved exactly what it was supposed to? But was it really necessary to make getting there so convoluted?

Once her office was clear, Abby settled in front of her computer. She'd realised that Quinn Beaumont would probably be living on the second floor with her, and she was tempted to do a little reading about him. However, she quickly decided against it. She already knew Quinn had a reputation, and she was used to working with people who had a less than perfect past. Abby had never made a habit of digging into her squad's history, so she wasn't about to start now.

Picking up the phone, she dialled the extension for Lisa, the administration assistant she shared with Mrs Barclay.

"Lisa, could you come to my office?" Abby said, when Lisa answered. Without waiting for a reply, she hung up and sorted the stack of invoices she needed to talk Lisa through.

"Told you I'd see you around," a familiar voice said.

Abby looked up, surprised. "Ellis," she said, quickly registering the scratch across his cheek and the large plaster on the side of his neck. "What are you doing here?"

"I don't suppose you have any cakes going spare?" he asked, his dark eyes studying her hopefully before scanning the room.

"I take it you like to come for the leftovers from the department head meeting?" Abby asked, summing up the situation neatly.

"Well, Mrs B knows I'm a growing boy," he said, his smile widening at the sight of the tea trolley.

"Boy?" Abby asked, raising her eyebrows. "You must be at least twenty-five."

"Actually, I'm twenty-four," he said, heading over to the trolley. "Can I?"

"Help yourself," Abby said. "As long as you take some out for Jiro and Carly as well." She'd recently been introduced to the head gardener and the other assistant.

"I will," Ellis said as he chewed on an enormous mouthful of Victoria sponge.

"What happened?" Abby asked, gesturing to his face and neck.

"Small disagreement with a bramble," he said.

As he neatly folded a napkin around the other treats in a way that made it clear he was practised at this particular activity, Lisa arrived.

"Sorry, the phone rang again just as I was coming through," she said, flustered. Her cheeks flushed as she spotted Ellis.

"See you later, Ellis," Abby said.

Ellis glanced at Lisa, his usually confident posture shifting slightly, hinting at an uncertainty that Abby wouldn't have expected in him. "Oh, you'll definitely see me later," he said, wiggling his eyebrows in a suggestive way that had Abby rolling her eyes. Ellis was definitely entertaining, but she'd worked with enough younger men to know that he was simply full of the bravado of youth.

Turning her attention back to Lisa, Abby resisted the urge to frown. Over the last week, Abby had discovered that Lisa was eminently capable, but her blush didn't seem to be dissipating.

"Sorry, Miss Smith," Lisa said, slipping into the chair opposite Abby's desk and opening her notebook.

Abby was relieved that Lisa had abandoned the unnecessary chatter she'd spent most of last week attempting. They needed to focus on the tasks at hand.

Once they were finished, Abby watched Lisa gather the documents. She was certainly enthusiastic about her work, but today she had been surprisingly subdued. Just as Abby was wondering if she should try to find out what was bothering her, Lisa left the room abruptly. Abby had seen enough people struggling with things in the military, and she knew that sometimes they were more willing to open up to someone they weren't close to.

Making up her mind, Abby followed the corridor towards Lisa's desk, just outside of Mrs Barclay's office. Just before she rounded the corner, the sound of voices drifted towards her.

"Honestly, she's a nightmare," Lisa was saying. "She's so busy ordering everyone around. She's clearly used to men just falling over themselves to do what she tells them."

"I thought she seemed nice enough," replied the other voice, which wasn't familiar to Abby.

"She doesn't even say hello or goodbye on the phone," Lisa said. "She just barks an order and hangs up."

"Oh, that doesn't sound fun," the other voice replied.

"I love this job, but I'm not sure I can cope with a whole summer like this," Lisa replied. "Thank God she's only temporary."

Stepping back as quietly as she could, Abby headed back to her own office. Was she the reason for Lisa's change of mood?

Thinking about their interactions over the last week, Abby remembered Lisa bounding into the office during the meetings that Mrs Beaumont had led — when had that enthusiasm dipped? Lisa had remained perfectly happy in the meetings late last week, when it had just been the two of them. It had only been today that she'd been so quiet.

Abby wanted to shake the conversation off and pretend that Lisa was only so upset with her because she was having a bad day, but she had led enough people over the years to know that response wouldn't help. She had to be open to the idea that she could do better.

Abby had known adjusting to civilian life was going to be hard. She just hadn't realised she was going to screw it up so badly.

CHAPTER SEVEN

Forcing a smile, Quinn let his bag drop onto the floor of the entrance hall and accepted Donna's hug.

"You'll be starving after your journey," she said. "Come through. I have some scones fresh out of the oven."

At the mention of his favourite treat, his smile slipped into something much more genuine. "Now, should I add the jam first or the cream?" Quinn asked, as he trailed after Donna through the familiar labyrinth of the house to the restaurant kitchen.

Her laugh seemed to surround him. The feeling of being home started to settle into his bones and helped him relax.

"I'll be leaving that debate to the good folks of Devon and Cornwall," Donna said, as he knew she would. "You just eat it however you think it tastes best."

Settling on the stool in the corner of the kitchen, Quinn took a bite of his scone. The kitchen was the perfect place to catch up with the rest of the household. Almost every member of the Rose Hall team came through at some time during the afternoon, and despite himself, Quinn enjoyed chatting with them. As Donna and her team moved from serving the many customers to cleaning up and preparing for the next day, Quinn made his excuses and went to collect his bag and find his mother.

Walking back through the house, he was briefly worried when he found that his bag was gone, before realising that Mr Heath had probably arranged for it to be moved up to his room in the family quarters. Upstairs, he discovered that everything had been unpacked and placed in the wardrobe and drawers. Even his washbag had been unpacked and the contents set out in the bathroom. While it was a thoughtful gesture, it made him roll his eyes. God forbid he have any kind of privacy. Pulling the door closed behind him and attempting to shrug off his frustration, he went in search of his mother.

Walking into the small kitchenette that the family used for meals when they couldn't mooch something from the kitchen downstairs, he was surprised to find a tall, slim woman, her red hair in a tidy ponytail. She was wearing a boxy trouser suit.

"Hello," Quinn said, knowing his surprise was clear in his tone.

The woman turned around, teaspoon in hand. Quinn took in large aqua-blue eyes and a complexion that was almost as pale as his own, although the woman's skin was a lot healthier in appearance than his own.

"Can I help you?" she asked.

"Who are you?" Quinn knew the question sounded rude, but he couldn't stop himself from blurting it out.

The woman frowned at his manner but didn't immediately answer. What was wrong with him? He was charming, everyone said so. In fact, he was so charming that his name and presence were enough to secure business for his friends. Where had that charm disappeared to? Perhaps being back here was more unsettling than he'd realised.

"You must be Beatrice's son?" the woman asked.

Frowning at her use of his mother's first name, Quinn nodded. "And you are?" he asked, deciding that as his charm had entirely abandoned him, he had no choice but to channel his best *lord of the manor* voice.

"I'm Abby Smith," she said. "I'm helping with the events over the summer."

Ah, he'd forgotten about that. "That still doesn't explain why you're up here," he said, leaning against the doorframe. His slipping manners were disconcerting him.

"I'm staying here," Abby said, turning to finish making her hot drink. Her movements were controlled — not graceful, like the way that his mother and Cordelia moved, but somehow bearing the same deep confidence. It was a strength Quinn envied.

With his thoughts distracted, it took a moment for Abby's answer to sink in. She was staying here? On the family floor? Did that mean he was going to have to deal with her for the rest of the summer? He wasn't sure he could deal with himself, never mind someone else.

Turning, Abby gave him a smile, one so real, so genuinely amused, that Quinn actually sucked in a breath. "It looks like we'll be seeing lots of each other over the next few months," she said, her eyes glinting.

It was clear that despite his attempts to exert his authority, Quinn had simply made an idiot of himself.

CHAPTER EIGHT

Abby watched Quinn Beaumont as he made his way through the staff who were gathered outside. Gone was the awkward man she'd met the evening before. In his place was someone who moved with a confidence that came with wealth and privilege, and the knowledge that the world would simply mould itself to your expectations. Grateful for the extra layer of her suit jacket, Abby resisted the urge to shiver in the coolness of the early spring morning.

Wearing a pair of chinos and a white shirt, Quinn's height was just as apparent as it had been last night. He had the sort of lean build that came from running rather than using a gym, and with his light brown hair pushed back from his face, he looked every inch the upper-class man he was. He was attractive enough that Abby understood why the press were so interested in his movements. Right now, he was far more the person she'd been expecting; today's apparent charm was more in keeping with a man who was regularly photographed living the society lifestyle of parties and other events. Somehow, though, the curt and clearly flustered man of the night before had seemed more real. Watching him, Abby reflected that Quinn didn't look like someone who had been in and out of rehab. The paleness of his complexion hinted at late nights, too much partying, and not enough time outdoors, but it didn't hide his handsome features.

Around him, faces lit up as he spoke to them. Abby realised she was witnessing a much-loved son returning home and wondered why he'd stayed away when he was clearly so adored here. Something about his manner didn't seem quite right, though. It was almost as if he was playing a part.

Before Abby could explore that train of thought any further, Beatrice Beaumont joined them, her three dogs swirling around her ankles as usual. Abby had to supress a grin when she took in the co-ordinated tracksuit Mrs Beaumont was wearing. It was much smarter, and clearly more tailored than your average tracksuit, but that didn't quell Abby's amusement at seeing the older woman in something other than her much-loved tweed. Turning her head in an attempt to make sure Mrs Beaumont didn't see her reaction, Abby caught sight of Quinn, the curl of his lip and the twinkle in his eye making her wonder if he was having the same thoughts as she was.

"Mother," he said, his voice richer and warmer that it had been when he'd spoken to Abby the night before. "Are you ill?"

Mrs Beaumont frowned. "No…" she said cautiously.

"But you're dressed in leisure wear!"

"Oh, you naughty boy," Mrs Beaumont said, giving her son a good-natured swipe on the arm. "Now, you didn't all have to come and see me off."

Her words were entirely at odds with her delighted expression. The fact that almost all of the staff had come to say goodbye before she was driven to the airport was obviously something that meant a great deal to her.

"We just wanted to make sure you actually went," Quinn said, causing a ripple of laughter in the assembled group.

Something inside of Abby warmed at the obvious love the Beaumonts had for each other. She'd spent a long time away from home herself, and watching Mrs Beaumont and Quinn gave her hope that her relationship with her own parents would strengthen — at least once her mum stopped trying to arrange her life.

As the taxi carried Beatrice away from Rose Hall and towards the airport, the gathered group began to scatter.

Ellis wandered over to Abby. "Would it be okay if we did the bedding areas outside your office window this morning?" he asked, placing a hand on her arm.

"That's fine," Abby said. "Thanks." As Ellis wandered away, Abby began to listen in on the conversation Quinn was having.

"What are your plans for today?" Mrs Barclay asked him.

"I could chat with you this morning and spend some time in the kitchen this afternoon," Quinn said. "I guess it would be sensible to get caught up on everything that's happening."

Abby tilted her head, sensing the reluctance in Quinn's tone. She wondered why he was making the suggestion.

"You don't want to get involved in boring work. Just relax and enjoy yourself. I'll save you some scones for when you want a snack," Donna said, before heading back into the building.

"Oh no, dear, there's no need for you to worry about any of that," Mrs Barclay added. "Everything is running smoothly." There was a finality to her tone, and she rushed away from Quinn before he could respond.

Just as Abby was about to turn and head off herself, the almost imperceptible slump in Quinn's posture made her pause. Before she could stop herself, she found her mouth opening. "As you aren't busy, I could do with a hand to work through your mother's event plans for the summer," she said, her voice casual, but with the steely undertone that turned her requests into orders. She could easily do the work on her own, but in the army she'd learned that one of the quickest ways to help the new recruits feel part of the team was to simply insist that their help was needed.

Quinn faced her, studying her intently, as though trying to work out how she had the nerve to essentially order him to do something. Abby simply held his gaze. She'd spent enough years dealing with drill instructors not to feel uncomfortable with people staring her down. However, there was something awkward about being the target of Quinn Beaumont's focus, something in the intensity of his brown eyes that made her understand exactly why so many women were happy to be photographed with him.

As the staring contest continued, Abby wondered if she'd screwed up by giving her new boss the impression she needed help, but she quickly shrugged that thought off. People here already seemed to have a negative view of her; it wasn't as if she could make things worse.

Finally, just as Abby was considering withdrawing the offer, Quinn nodded.

"Lead the way," he said.

CHAPTER NINE

Standing in the doorway of his mother's office, Quinn watched Abby as she worked at his mother's desk. Her dark red hair was in a bun so tight that he wondered how it wasn't causing her discomfort.

Grateful for her distraction, he took a moment to organise his thoughts. He wasn't really sure why he was here. He didn't want to run his family's estate. He definitely didn't want a job that he hadn't earned. When his mother had coerced him into spending the summer here, he'd sworn to himself he would do as little as possible, determined not to get sucked into things. But it had still hurt to be dismissed by Donna and Mrs Barclay so quickly. So when Abby had asked for his assistance — or rather, ordered him to help her — he had desperately wanted to say yes.

Abby raised her head, her gaze meeting his. "Are you planning to stand brooding in the doorway all day?" she asked. "We have a lot to get through."

Resisting the urge to shuffle in as if he was still a child, Quinn stepped into the room, forcing his face into the expression he used when Charlie wheeled him out to woo clients. "What are you struggling with?" he asked.

Abby raised an eyebrow and ignored his question. "I've just finished the planner," she said. "You take this end, and we can put it up on the wall." She stepped close enough for a flowery scent to reach his nose, before thrusting one end of a huge roll of paper into his hand and stepping back, unfurling as she went.

"You did this by hand?" Quinn asked, staring at the planner once it was up. The grid was so perfect and the text so neat that you'd have to have been very close to it to realise it hadn't been created on a computer.

"Yes," Abby replied. "Now, let's go through the tasks that need completing this week and divvy them up."

Quinn turned and frowned at her expectant expression.

"Sorry," Abby said, not looking the slightest bit sorry. "Do you have plans to work with any of the other departments? If so, how much time will you have to work in events this week?"

Quinn knew he should find her high-handed manner irritating, but something about her assumption that he would be busy working felt good. He couldn't remember the last time anyone had had expectations of him. Even his mother didn't really expect him to do anything. Yet Abby, who knew nothing about him other than whatever she'd read in the press, was simply assuming that he'd be fully involved in everything that was going on.

Quinn snorted at the thought; if she'd read any of the press coverage about him, there was no way she would be thinking he could add any value to her work.

Abby tilted her head at the sound, and Quinn realised she'd been waiting for his response.

"I, um … I think I'll focus on events for now," Quinn said, not sure why he sounded so tentative. "If that's okay with you, Miss Smith?"

"Of course," she said. "It will be great to have the help."

Before he could say anything further or retract his suggestion, Abby turned and pointed to a section of the planner. "Our first event is the outdoor cinema weekend. This list of vendors will need contacting," she said. "I'll start at the top of the list, you start at the bottom, and we can tick each one off as it's completed. You use the landline and I'll use the mobile." She sat down at the round table and opened her notepad before handing him a stack of files.

Holding the stack, Quinn stepped closer to the list on the wall and swallowed hard. The array of businesses that were involved in the event made his head spin. It was a cinema event, surely that meant a movie and some popcorn. How could they possibly need so much stuff?

"Why don't you listen in on my first call, just to refresh your memory on everything you need to cover?" Abby suggested.

Quinn nodded and sat opposite her.

She dialled a number, and as she waited for someone to answer the call, she gestured for him to grab a notebook and pen. He resisted the urge to roll his eyes. While her level of organisation was quite impressive, it was clear it came from a need to control everything.

Abby started her call. After a cursory greeting, she quickly moved on to discussing the logistical requirements of the day, from arrival time, location of their pitch, and restocking times during the weekend, through to insurance requirements and the post-event clean-up protocol. She handled the call with a rigid efficiency that was impressive, if a little terrifying.

Frantically making notes, it took Quinn a moment to realise she had finished talking.

"Those files," Abby said, gesturing to the stack she'd given him, "are for the vendors towards the bottom of the list. Each file has the details you need for the calls with them."

Quinn nodded his understanding, staring at the pile as though they were venomous snakes.

"Great," Abby said, either oblivious to, or determined to ignore, his obvious panic.

Still convinced this was a terrible idea, but for some reason unwilling to disappoint Abby and her unnerving confidence in him, Quinn moved to his mother's desk and picked up the phone, dialling the first vendor in his pile.

"Okay," Abby said a few hours later. "That's enough for today."

Blinking, Quinn looked up from the notes he was making after the call he'd just finished with the vegan food truck company. A quick glance at the grandfather clock in the corner let him know it was almost six o'clock. How had that happened? The day had passed so quickly; he was sure he wouldn't have even remembered lunch if Donna hadn't sent Ellis up with a tray of sandwiches and tea.

"There's still so much to do," Quinn said.

"There is," Abby said. "But there would still be a lot more to do if you hadn't been here."

Something inside of Quinn seemed to balloon at her statement. Each call had taken him much longer to complete than Abby, mostly because he found it impossible to simply direct the conversation to the business at hand, but he'd really enjoyed chatting to the different suppliers and he felt like he'd achieved something worthwhile. The thought took him by surprise. When was the last time he had felt like he'd achieved anything?

CHAPTER TEN

Friday morning started well enough. Abby, as usual, was the first to appear in the office she shared with Quinn, but she started to worry once ten o'clock came and went without any sign of him. Torn between concern that something had happened to him, and irritation that he hadn't bothered to turn up or even let her know what was happening, Abby took a deep breath.

Quinn's every action in their first few days working together had made it apparent that while he was a quick learner, he wasn't remotely used to hard work. After forcing herself to concentrate on her own work for another half an hour, Abby decided she'd had enough. She was going to have to track him down. Whether he realised it or not, Quinn was a man who needed a purpose, and Abby wasn't about to let him fail — at least not without him making the decision to do so consciously.

Smiling at the members of staff that she passed, Abby realised that it would have been far quicker to find out if anyone had seen Quinn in the kitchen before she schlepped all the way upstairs to his room, but she didn't want anyone else knowing that he hadn't made it through a full week without slipping up.

Once she was in the family quarters, Abby felt a little awkward about banging on Quinn's bedroom door, but she did it anyway. After all, she'd spent years waking her colleagues up and disturbing them in their private quarters.

She waited a full minute before banging on the door again. It was the sort of knock that reverberated through any space, the sort of knock that had been honed over years of having to wake people up after nights of heavy drinking, or extended periods where sleep had been a luxury in short supply. Abby waited again, and this time the silence was broken by faint sounds of movement on the other side of the door.

"What?" Quinn demanded, his usually soft voice rough with sleep as he swung the door open.

"It's almost eleven," Abby said, arms folded, her posture ramrod-straight as she waited for the meaning of her words to sink in. She attempted to keep her eyes off his bare chest, the dim light of the corridor seeming to highlight every line of his muscles.

For a moment, Quinn simply blinked at her, confusion etched into his features, before understanding finally transformed them. "Oh, God," he said, his entire body seeming to slump. "I'm so sorry."

Despite the obvious regret on his face, Abby didn't respond. Instead, deploying another of her favourite tactics, she simply stared at him, waiting for him to fill the silence with whatever excuses would be dredged up. His gaze fixed on the ground, he pushed his hair out of his face, and Abby resisted the urge to smile at the way it simply flopped straight back down.

"I really am terribly sorry," Quinn said, straightening as his gaze met hers. His shoulders squared. "There is no excuse for letting you down like this. I will be in the office as soon as possible, and I promise it will not happen again."

Abby realised that if it hadn't been for all the practice she'd had at hiding her emotions, her surprise at Quinn's response would have been obvious. In all her years, she'd never had someone take responsibility so quickly and so directly. He had even avoided making pointless excuses. She nodded her acceptance and turned away, grateful to escape before her façade of indifference at the man dressed in only a pair of pyjama bottoms slipped.

By the middle of the next week, Abby was pleased to find that she and Quinn had found a comfortable rhythm. After his lie-in on Friday morning, he had been in the office on time, or even early, every day. Abby sensed a change in him, as though he was actually welcoming the responsibilities of working at Rose Hall. Everything was so well organised that she had even been able to start working on the next set of events. Quinn's easy manner made him much better at dealing with the vendors than she was. He wasn't any more efficient than her, but his friendliness meant that he was quicker to secure their agreement to each of the requirements that Beatrice Beaumont had failed to mention to them as part of the original contracts and arrangements.

If Quinn thought it was strange that Abby had been employed to do all of this, but was regularly insisting that she needed him to continue helping, he didn't say anything. Abby found she was actually enjoying his company, and he certainly seemed to be enjoying his days as well. In the army, being direct and authoritative had been essential, and she was finding it hard to modify her approach now she was a civilian. The fact that the rest of the staff seemed to work so differently to her was something that she was still struggling with, so it was a welcome relief to work with Quinn, who seemed to enjoy being told what to do.

"Miss Smith, I've got the cinema people on the line. They want to double-check something about the power supply. Do you have their file?" Quinn asked, holding the phone to his shoulder, despite the fact Abby had shown him how to put people on hold.

"I'm pretty sure I gave that to you earlier," she said. He frowned and shuffled the array of folders spread across the desk.

Standing, Abby covered the short distance to Beatrice's desk, and started searching. She quickly found the file in question and flicked through it. Finding the section that contained the technical details, she opened it and placed it so Quinn could easily see the required details. She pointed to the section that covered power supply, so he could respond to any questions he might face.

"I'm just going to see Barry and make sure he will be ready for Friday," Quinn said, once he was off the phone. With Abby's nod of approval, he headed out to meet the estate butcher — Rose Hall had successfully launched their own organic meat products a few years earlier.

Working through her task list for the day, Abby decided to follow Quinn's lead and go and speak to Mrs Barclay in person. It would be quicker to just call her, but Abby was determined to try to improve her own approach.

After a lovely catch-up with Mrs Barclay, Abby made her way back towards the office she shared with Quinn, laden with a huge stack of files that held the previous year's details. She found herself pausing in the corridor again at the sound of her name.

"You can't actually like Abby?" The disbelief in Lisa's voice was coming through clearly.

Abby couldn't understand how Lisa could be so pleasant to her face when the younger woman obviously didn't like her at all. In the army, everyone just said their piece and got on with it.

"She might seem okay," Lisa said with a laugh, "but she's always barking orders, and she's got the men completely wrapped around her finger."

Abby frowned. She might not be making the best of impressions on the team, but on the whole, things were going okay. It seemed like Lisa specifically had a problem with her.

"I know she can be a bit sharp, but I'm sure she doesn't mean anything by it. Anyway, what do you mean?" the other voice said, clearly female, but not one Abby recognised.

"Well, she's got Ellis running all sorts of errands for her. Do you know he takes her tea trays through to her? He works in the garden. Why does she think she can make him wait on her as well? Now she's even got Mr Beaumont working for her. He's the heir to the estate, and she's managed to persuade him to do her job so she can take it easy," Lisa said, her tone betraying the depth of her resentment.

Abby's heart sank. She knew full well that she'd never asked, or even hinted that Ellis should bring her tea trays. Abby suspected the lad had appointed himself as the delivery person because he knew he'd get to snag some of the treats.

"But…" the other voice began hesitantly, "surely Mr Beaumont would just say no if he didn't want to do something? She couldn't make him do it."

Abby let out a silent breath; at least the person Lisa was talking to wasn't completely agreeing with her.

"I don't think she has to make either of them, if you catch my drift," Lisa said. "Let's be honest, some women just use their gender to get what they want."

Silence greeted that poisonous remark. Abby wasn't sure if Lisa's companion had been struck mute, or if the pair had moved away.

The sound of a cough behind her made Abby jump, but fortunately her reflexes meant she was able to keep the stack of files from slipping out of her hands. Unfortunately, that became the least of her concerns when she realised who had been behind her. Quinn's expression was so solemn that Abby couldn't convince herself he hadn't overheard the same conversation she had. It was embarrassing enough that someone thought so little of her, without him knowing it.

"Are you —" Quinn began, concern so deeply etched into his features that Abby wished she could disappear.

"Mrs Barclay has given us the files from last year," Abby said, interrupting before he could complete the question.

Thankfully he took the hint, and they were soon back in Beatrice's office and settled down at their separate workstations.

Abby realised that she wanted to speak to her brother, Rob. He was the one person she knew who would be appropriately outraged for her, without it actually worrying him. Perhaps she could make an excuse to go outside and call Rob; it would certainly help to get this off her chest. Picking up her mobile, Abby quickly responded to the latest message from her old team, then stood.

"Do you have the file for the cinema people?" Quinn asked.

The question threw her thoughts off track. She crossed the room to Quinn's desk and flicked through the files again.

"I definitely saw that one earlier," she said. Quinn urgently needed to find a more organised way of working.

Quickly coming across the folder she was looking for, she handed it to him with a smile, trying to ignore the careful way he was watching her. Not usually one for self-doubt, Abby found herself wondering if Quinn believed she was somehow manipulating him with her non-existent feminine wiles.

"Thanks," Quinn said, his gaze dropping to the folder.

Letting out a breath she hadn't realised she'd been holding, Abby returned to her own seat and focused on work, silently wondering whether they would ever get back to the easiness they had been sharing.

"So, you have a penchant for rom-coms?" Quinn asked a few moments later. He was standing next to her.

Abby frowned at him, wondering where the random but accurate remark had come from.

"My apologies, you left this on my desk and I glanced at your screen without meaning to," Quinn said, holding her mobile out to her and pushing his hair back awkwardly. "I don't make a habit of invading people's privacy."

Reaching out to take her phone back, Abby smiled. "I adore rom-coms — the mistake I made was letting my squad find out."

"Your squad?" Quinn asked, brows furrowing. "Is that like your crew or your fam, or whatever the kids call their friendship group these days?"

"I'm not trying to pretend I'm young and hip," Abby said, laughing at the way the words sounded in his smooth, rich tone. "I was a sergeant in the army."

"Oh," Quinn said, his head tilting to one side, as though trying to fit this new bit of information with whatever impression he'd formed of her. "When did you leave?"

"Two months ago," Abby replied, pleased that he hadn't slipped into the standard responses she was used to getting — the kind that somehow managed to express surprise, as though people felt she clearly couldn't hack the military.

"So how are you finding the transition to civilian life?" Quinn asked, surprising her again. The only other person who'd asked her this particular question was Abby's friend

Tess but, given that Tess's husband Mike had been part of Abby's squad when he'd died on active duty, Tess had a unique insight into army life.

"Not as easy as I'd hoped," Abby said.

"We should make a pact," Quinn said, his expression serious. "You help me get the rest of the team to take me seriously, and I'll help you get used to us civilians."

Abby opened her mouth to object, but before she could respond, Quinn continued.

"Look, I'll be straight with you, I don't want to be here," he said, crouching down next to her, his face level with hers. "My mother strong-armed me into doing it, but that doesn't mean I want the staff here to think I'm as useless as they clearly do. I'm perfectly aware that you could do all of this without me." He gestured around the room, before pushing his hair back. "I'm also aware that you heard exactly how people reacted when I offered to help out."

Abby gave him a wry smile. "And you heard just what they think of me," she said, managing to force the words out. Somehow, his willingness to be open with her made her want to share in return.

He wrinkled his nose. "I thought you were going to try and persuade me that they don't think I'm useless."

"If you want empty reassurances, you've come to the wrong person," Abby said, smiling to take the sting out of her words. "They think you're still the little boy they knew. Something that clearly isn't the case, so it won't take them long to see how capable you are now. Unfortunately, I'm used to working with people who give and take orders, not people who meander around things. I'm pretty sure my problem will take a lot more fixing than yours."

"Well, when you put it like that…" Quinn stood and gave her that charming smile that usually made everyone around him melt, but always made Abby wonder what he was hiding from. "I simply need to be myself and they will all see how wonderfully capable I am, but you are clearly a hopeless case."

"That's a bit much," Abby began, bristling.

"If you want empty reassurances, you've come to the wrong person," Quinn said, throwing her statement back at her. This time, his smile was different; just one lip curled upwards and his eyes lit up. It looked more sincere and intimate.

Abby stared at him for a moment before bursting into laughter. "Very well played, Mr Beaumont."

"Indeed," he said. "So, do we have a deal?"

"Are you sure you want to agree to such an imbalanced arrangement?" Abby asked.

"Well, Miss Smith, if you will stop calling me Mr Beaumont, I am prepared to take on such an arduous challenge," Quinn said, holding out his hand.

Standing and clasping his strong hand with her own, Abby nodded. "I'm in, but you need to stop calling me Miss Smith as well."

CHAPTER ELEVEN

Crossing the area that had been set aside for those attendees who had opted to bring their own chairs and blankets, rather than pay the premium for the luxury seats provided, Quinn strode towards Abby. Despite the fact they'd both been working flat out since six o'clock in the morning, her boxy suit remained immaculate. Even her hair was still contained in the bun she wore every day. She looked entirely comfortable amongst the variety of estate and vendor staff who were milling back and forth. Quinn wondered if he'd ever find that level of self-assurance.

"I hope that doesn't come to anything," Abby said, lifting her chin towards the ever-darkening sky.

"I'm surprised a bit of rain would bother you," Quinn said.

"I was hoping we'd get a few last-minute customers and sell the final tickets."

"Tonight is the only showing that isn't sold out, though."

Abby wrinkled her nose, and Quinn knew she was attempting to hold in her frustration. "I know," she said. "Still, nothing to be done about it now. I need to go and talk to Andy." She nodded towards the huge inflatable screen that Andy, its owner, was securing with multiple guy lines.

"Okay," Quinn said, one side of his lip curling as he continued. "Now, before you go over there, I think you should practise saying hello."

Tilting her head to one side, Abby stared at him, but he was determined to leave her with a smile on her face.

"Firstly, you have to smile; that's that thing where you lift the sides of your mouth. Then you have to say hello, but make sure you use a cheerful tone." Despite his attempts to keep his tone serious, the sight of Abby's blank expression shifting into a terrible attempt at a frown meant he couldn't keep it up.

"Thank you for that very important lesson. Could we cover the rest of the conversation I need to have as well?" she asked, clearly amused.

"Baby steps, Abby. I'm not sure we have enough time for me to make sure you handle an entire conversation well. For now, just remember to keep those feminine wiles in check."

"Understood. I'll come back for that lesson another time. For now, shall I explain to you how to check the items on that list off?"

"Oh, yes please," Quinn said. "I don't want to let the staff see that I'm just as incompetent as they think I am."

Any trace of amusement in Abby's expression disappeared. "You are not incompetent," she said, her voice firm enough that Quinn could well understand how she kept trained soldiers under control.

He simply raised his eyebrow at her. He wasn't stupid. He had just turned thirty and his only gainful employment to date had been by virtue of the fact that he knew a lot of high-profile people and could be quite charming when he could be bothered. "I've needed you to show me literally everything," he said.

"And?"

"What do you mean, and? I'm a grown man and can't do anything," he said, knowing his voice was raised but not able to control it. Luckily, he managed to stop himself from flinging his arms up in frustration.

"Now you're just feeling sorry for yourself," Abby said firmly, rolling her eyes. "Look around you. Saying you can't do anything is patently untrue. A huge amount of what you see here is because of your hard work."

He frowned but made himself look around. She was right, he had played his part in getting the event up and running. "But you could have done this without me, and you had to tell me what to do," he said, aware he was starting to sound whiney.

"You are a hopeless case," Abby said. "Of course I could have done this; so could lots of people. And yes, of course I had to show you what to do. Do you think it only counts if you are the only person who can do something? Do you think there are people out there who don't need someone to show them how to do something for the first time?"

She hadn't become any louder as she'd spoken, but there was something in the urgency of her voice that made Quinn pause. Unable to take the intensity of her pale blue gaze, he looked around again and wondered. Was Abby right? Was he being too hard on himself? Sure, he was embarrassingly old to have needed so much help, but he realised he could do this again without needing someone to show him. Okay, well maybe not all of it, but at least the bits he'd already done.

Turning back to Abby, he gave her a small smile, not sure how to articulate the thoughts that were swirling around in his head. She was watching him carefully, her own expression shifting into something that seemed a little sad.

"I told you I had the easier end of the deal," she said, turning on her heel before he could respond.

CHAPTER TWELVE

Taking a large bite of the hotdog he'd just had handed to him, Quinn let out a groan of satisfaction. "Calling this a hotdog doesn't do it justice," he said.

"I'm not giving it some fancy name," Barry, the estate butcher, replied with a laugh. "It's a sausage in a bread roll, even if it is one of the best sausages you'll ever find, and the rolls are Honey and Rose Bakery's finest."

"I'm not going to argue with you," Quinn said, taking another bite.

Barry served another of the steady stream of customers who'd been coming up to the food truck all evening.

"It's great how everyone mucks in," Quinn said, throwing his napkin into the bin as Barry came back over.

"We're a family here," Barry said. "But you know that, you're actually part of the family."

Quinn shrugged. He supposed he should have known, but perhaps the fact he'd always felt like the kid at the table meant he'd never noticed how good that sense of extended family could be.

It was the last night of the cinema weekend, and he'd spent the last few days watching everyone work together. If it hadn't been for the department heads enforcing breaks, he suspected half the team wouldn't have stopped at all. For the first time in a long time, Quinn felt like he was a part of something that mattered, and for a few seconds the thought that he wouldn't mind staying seemed to tighten around his mind.

He passed a few minutes chatting to Barry about the event, Barry's husband George, and life in general, before making his excuses so he could go and find Abby. He'd realised that she'd been up and about long before him every morning, and she'd been the last to call it quits every night. He wasn't sure how she managed it.

Picking his way around the edge of the rapidly filling viewing areas, he smiled at the sight of Abby, her head bent as she listened to something Mrs Barclay was saying. He knew the older woman wasn't planning to stay for the evening, so she was likely to be regaling Abby with a list of things that needed to happen at the end of the event.

"What mischief are you two plotting?" Quinn asked, his tone teasing as he stopped next to the pair.

"Oh, all sorts of things, but we couldn't possibly tell you," Abby replied, turning to him with a smile that added to Quinn's pleasure at being home.

Mrs Barclay's expression was more serious. "Don't be silly, Quinn," she said, her tone the same as it had been twenty years ago, when she'd been reprimanding him for some infraction or other. "You're the one who's most likely to be up to something you shouldn't be."

Quinn focused on keeping his expression light, letting his Beaumont smile hide just how deeply her words had stung. "Not these days," he said, trying not to let the old resentments grow. "Abby's keeping me in check."

Mrs Barclay turned to Abby, her expression shifting to one of approval. "Excellent," she said.

"Actually, Quinn doesn't need anyone to keep him in check. He's been brilliant," Abby said, any amusement from her initial exchange with him gone, her features shifting into that blank look he disliked so much. "I'm lucky to have been working with him."

Quinn's weariness and hurt at Mrs Barclay's familiar response seemed to ease back at Abby's reaction. She was holding Mrs Barclay's gaze, as though she was challenging her. Quinn tried to think of some witty remark that would ease the tension.

"We'll see you at the managers' meeting tomorrow," Abby said before Quinn could think of anything, her clipped tone firmly back in place.

Quinn knew he should be giving Abby the look, the one they'd agreed he'd use whenever she was slipping into her military style, but he found he couldn't. Actually, he didn't want to. He might not like the fact that, despite what he had achieved with Abby's help, it had made no difference to Mrs Barclay's opinion of him, but he definitely liked that Abby wasn't letting it go unchecked.

"Yes, I hope this evening goes well," Mrs Barclay said, turning and walking around the side of the building towards the staff car park.

"The rest of the weekend has gone well, why on earth wouldn't this evening?" Abby said, the words muttered so quietly that Quinn realised he wasn't supposed to have heard. Deciding to redirect the conversation to the reason he'd come over to see her, he forced his smile to retreat and leant over Abby's shoulder to look at the form on her clipboard.

"You've done everything on your list," he said.

"Yes, but I still want to do a walkthrough and make sure everything is back in proper order before we let this evening's customers in."

"I've done that," he said.

"Thank you, that's a huge help." The sudden warmth in her voice eased the last of his hurt, and the realisation that she trusted him made his chest swell.

"My pleasure. Shall we get them to open the gates?"

Over the next couple of hours, the grounds were filled with customers milling around. The provided seating was padded deckchairs with small tables for people to rest their snacks and drinks. The supplier had decorated the area with bunting in simple spring colours. Thin strips of neon lighting marked the edges of the seating area and as dusk began to fall, they led the way to the bank of luxury Portaloos that were tucked neatly out of sight behind a row of conifers.

"So, are you going to relax and watch this one?" Quinn asked Abby.

"No. Well, I'm not saying I won't keep an eye on the screen, but I really can't justify sitting and watching a movie when everyone else is still working so hard," she replied, gesturing around her.

"But it's a rom-com. They're your favourite."

"I do love them, but do you want to know a secret?" she said, leaning slightly closer.

Nodding, Quinn closed the gap between them further.

"I would have liked the time to watch this afternoon's film," Abby said, her face scrunching up as though admitting to something terrible.

"*Tangled?*" he asked. "Isn't that a kids' film?"

"I know. But what's not to love? It's a princess movie about a princess who can, and does, save herself."

Even in the dim lighting, Quinn could see Abby's cheeks pinkening. He'd begun to believe that her self-confidence was so deeply rooted that nothing fazed her, and while that was incredibly attractive, it was nice to see this side of her as well.

CHAPTER THIRTEEN

Most of the vendors had packed up and left. Only the cinema people needed to return in the morning, so they could safely pull all the guy ropes up in the daylight. Abby waved the last of the Rose Hall team home, with reassurances that the rest of the clean-up could wait until the next day. The satisfaction of a successful weekend would sustain her for a little longer as she got another couple of areas finished, and then she'd call it a night as well.

"You've just convinced the rest of the team to go home because this can all wait until the morning," Quinn said, standing in her path as she started to head towards her first target.

"I know," Abby said. "But they looked exhausted."

"So do you."

"Thanks." She laughed.

"You know what I mean. At least take a break before you do anything else."

She raised her eyebrows at him, not sure if it was worth taking a break at one o'clock in the morning when she only planned to do another half hour or so.

"Come on, if you don't take a break, I won't feel like I can."

At his words, she noticed the black shadows under his eyes. Despite the fact he'd started much later in the day than she had, it was clear he wasn't used to putting in these sorts of hours. Years of time spent on exercise and active duty meant Abby was practised at going for anything up to forty-eight hours without much rest, which meant a long weekend with limited sleep was barely noticeable, but she wasn't about to run Quinn into the ground because of that.

"Okay," she said. "Let's have a drink and see if we feel like doing any more of this afterwards."

"Come with me," Quinn said.

Abby followed him, smiling as she realised they were making their way towards the deckchairs.

"Here," Quinn said, gesturing to a pair of chairs that were positioned in the middle of the area. On the little table between them was a flask, two mugs and a Tupperware box. "You sit. I'll be back in just a minute."

Abby did as instructed, sighing as she sank into the chair. After the hustle and bustle of the last few days, the silence that surrounded her was calming.

Suddenly, a familiar tune and voice filled the air. Opening her eyes, she smiled. The screen was filled with the opening scene from *Tangled*.

"How did you make this happen?" Abby asked when Quinn sank into the chair next to her.

"I didn't want you to miss out completely, and Andy showed me how it all works before he went."

"Andy's okay with us using his equipment?"

"Yes. Now shush and watch the movie. Some of us haven't seen it before."

Eyes fixed firmly on the screen, Abby tried to concentrate on the movie she loved so much, rather than letting her thoughts drift to the fact that no one had ever done anything so thoughtful for her. Giving a small shiver, she sank further into her chair. Despite the fact it had been in the low twenties during the day, it was still only spring, and any warmth had long since vanished.

"Here," Quinn said, passing her a blanket. "And we've got hot chocolate if you fancy some?"

"That would be amazing."

Sipping her drink, Abby realised that Quinn must have had Donna or one of her team save some before they'd closed up the kitchen for the night, as they'd been doing a roaring trade all weekend.

Abby allowed herself a sideways glance at Quinn. He wasn't like most of the men she knew. His lean physique was toned, but without the broad muscles of the men she was used to working with. He had a casual grace that gave the impression of someone extraordinarily comfortable in his own skin, and yet she'd seen enough glimpses of his insecurities to know that wasn't accurate. As he pushed his hair out of his face, she studied his profile. The only imperfection on his classically handsome face was a bump on his nose, where it looked as if it had been broken at some stage. Yet somehow it seemed to enhance his looks, making him seem more real.

Shaking the irrelevant thought off, she turned her attention back to the screen and let the movie absorb her. She wasn't going to let her thoughts stray in that direction.

Blinking repeatedly, Abby realised the closing credits had roused her. She wasn't sure when she'd fallen asleep, but she suspected she'd missed most of the film. Suddenly remembering the hot chocolate, she tried to work out how much of a mess she'd made spilling it.

Aware her left hand wasn't empty, she squeezed, her sleep-addled brain registering the hand holding hers as she did so.

Smiling awkwardly, Quinn slipped his hand out of hers.

Looking around, Abby realised her mug was sitting on the small table between her and Quinn's chair. How had they been holding hands? Quinn would have had to lean over quite awkwardly to do that thanks to the cocooning nature of the chairs, and she definitely didn't remember anything that would explain the contact.

"I can't believe I fell asleep. Thank you for sorting my drink out." Abby's words were stilted as she tried to ignore how cold she felt now that Quinn wasn't holding her hand anymore.

"It was my pleasure," Quinn said. "And I'm not at all surprised you fell asleep. You have barely stopped for the last four days."

"I'm used to long hours and little rest."

He looked at her for a minute, as though trying to decide what to say. Abby forced herself to hold his gaze.

"I assume you don't sleep a lot because of the nightmares," Quinn said, his tone casual, but the stillness of his features suggested he wasn't sure this was an acceptable direction to take the conversation.

This time, Abby couldn't hold his gaze. The only person who knew about the dreams that had plagued her since she'd left the army was her brother, and that was because he'd refused to be fobbed off once he'd heard her cry out in her sleep. The longer she slept, the worse those dreams became. Everyone but Rob simply accepted the excuse that her years in the army meant she didn't need much sleep anymore.

"You don't have to say anything," Quinn said, his words quiet. "Just know that I'm here if you do want to talk."

Abby swallowed hard, blinking back the tears that threatened. This wasn't a subject she wanted to discuss, but something warm flickered inside at Quinn's offer. Shaking her head, she found she couldn't meet his eyes.

"That's fine, but if you change your mind, I'm here," he said, before sinking back into his chair. "I have to admit, I completely understand why you love this film."

"Who was your favourite character?" Abby asked, gratefully grabbing onto Quinn's tactful change of subject.

"Oh, definitely Maximus."

"Ah, the cheeky horse. I should have guessed that."

"What's that supposed to mean?" Quinn said, turning to face her.

Abby laughed at his expression of mock annoyance. The back and forth reminded her of the fun she'd had with her old colleagues and made her feel more at home than she had in months.

CHAPTER FOURTEEN

The managers' meeting went without a hitch. Just as Abby was gathering up her papers, Quinn cleared his throat, drawing everyone's attention.

"As the house will be open every day from the end of the month, I have arranged a barbecue for all the staff and their families next Monday afternoon," he said, smiling at the assembled group.

"Why don't I know about this?" Barry said, frowning.

"I promise we will be using Rose Hall Butchery produce," Quinn said, winking. "I've arranged for someone else to do the cooking, though, so you can relax for a change."

"But it's such short notice, people's families will be working or at school," Mrs Barclay said. She wasn't frowning, but her expression was severe enough to convey to everyone in the room that she disapproved. "And there will be lots of clean-up work to do."

"We'll start mid-afternoon and carry on through the evening, and as the garden doesn't open on a Monday or Tuesday at the moment, everyone can relax and enjoy themselves without an early start the next day," Quinn said, his voice calm. "And, most importantly, I've made arrangements so none of the staff have to do anything to clean up afterwards."

Abby smiled with pride. He'd approached her with the idea of doing something nice for the staff a few days earlier, and after bouncing ideas around he'd spoken to his mum. With Beatrice's approval, Quinn had taken full responsibility for organising the impromptu event. Abby knew exactly how nervous he'd been before sharing the news with the team today, and she was impressed with how well he'd hidden that.

"Well, thank you, Quinn," Mr Heath said. "I'm sure the teams will be delighted."

Watching Quinn trying to wave off the thanks of the assembled group, Abby found herself unable to look away. The pallor he'd arrived with was entirely gone now. The light tan that had started building as he'd spent more time working outdoors was replaced by a deep pink as everyone spoke over each other, determined to let him know how much they appreciated the gesture. Catching her eye, Quinn gave her a pleading look. Abby shrugged, as though to tell him he should just suck it up and enjoy it. After letting him suffer for a few more moments, she decided to rescue him.

"Okay, everyone, that's enough chatter, back to work now," she said, tapping her watch deliberately.

The sharp looks that were directed her way made her want to squirm, but she held firm. They would all have plenty of work to do this week if they were going to have an early finish next Monday and a late start the morning after.

"Just when you think she's getting better," someone said, the words drifting over and making her jaw tighten.

She'd thought she was getting better as well, but telling people it was time to get back to work wasn't wrong, especially when they were loitering in her office and making it impossible for her to get on. Maybe they needed to toughen up if simply having the truth pointed out to them set them on edge.

Quinn started to move towards her as the rest of the management team began to leave, his expression making it clear he'd heard the same thing she had, but she wasn't in the mood for another lesson in how she was getting it wrong. After missing the film with her nap last night, she hadn't managed much more than another forty minutes' sleep last night, and the efforts of the last few days were catching up with her.

Turning her attention to the door, she watched as Mrs Barclay and Donna walked out, the last ones to leave the room.

"It's going to be a disaster," Donna said.

"I know. What does the boy think he's doing, trying to organise something like that?" Mrs Barclay said.

"Well, hopefully it'll show him he's better leaving Rose Hall work to the professionals."

"I'm —" Mrs Barclay began, but the pair had moved too far for their words to be heard anymore.

Abby turned to see an ashen-faced Quinn, all his earlier enthusiasm gone. "Ignore them," she said. "They'll see just how wrong they are when everything goes well."

"Will you check the plans for me?" Quinn asked, not meeting her eyes.

"No," Abby said, keeping her tone soft despite her refusal.

For a moment Quinn stood, silent and motionless, before striding to the door and pushing it closed. "What do you mean, no?" he asked, his tone sharp. "You said you'd help me show them I'm not useless."

Abby turned and held his gaze, determined that he would understand just how strongly she meant her next words. "I am helping you."

"No, you are not," he said, his voice rising as he thrust his hand into his hair, his brown eyes darkening. "You have literally just said you won't check my plans."

"I am not going to check your plans, Quinn," she said. "You've thought of everything, and you've done an amazing job organising the barbecue. You should trust yourself."

He opened his mouth but shut it again. After doing this a couple of times, he threw his hands in the air. "I'm only asking you to double-check," he all but shouted, turning on his heel and throwing the door open before she could reply.

Abby watched him go, swallowing the need to call him back and tell him she would do it. She knew from experience that the only way he'd start to believe he was competent was if she let him do this without needing someone to approve his work. He'd covered everything she'd have suggested when he'd made his list during their brainstorming. Taking a deep breath, Abby strengthened her resolve. She suspected this was going to make the next week difficult, but she was more than capable of dealing with a grumpy colleague for a few days.

"Do you have the details for the costumier for the historical week?" Quinn asked, his voice clipped.

Abby resisted the urge to sigh; her predictions of a difficult week had been spot on. Quinn had essentially sulked for the entire time, keeping his interactions with her to the bare minimum.

"Of course," she replied, refusing to let her response reflect her frustration. She stood, and lifting the folder from her desk, she carried it to him. "How are you getting on with your list?"

"Fine," he said, not looking at her as he took the folder from her hands.

Rolling her eyes, she stepped back and gratefully answered her mobile, which had begun ringing.

"Hi, Tess," she said after checking the screen.

"Hi, Abby," Tess said. "Is now a bad time?"

"Not at all."

"I just wanted to let you know that Sam, Finn and I can make it on Monday if that's still okay?"

"That's brilliant," Abby said, pleased that she'd have company that actually wanted to spend time with her on Monday. She'd initially thought she wouldn't invite anyone, and had instead planned to use the time to get to know the rest of the team better. But as the week had gone on, she'd heard everyone else talking about bringing their partners, parents or friends, and she'd realised she didn't want to be the only one alone. Abby idly wondered who Quinn was inviting.

"Can we add three to the guest list for Monday?" Abby asked, after hanging up on Tess.

Quinn looked up sharply, giving a terse nod before turning his attention back to the file in front of him.

As he was working on the upcoming historical week, Abby focused on her own work. The day-to-day opening of the house and gardens were covered by the rest of the team at Rose Hall, but there were still another half dozen events to get through before her contract came to an end.

Staring at the page in front of her without seeing the words, Abby's thoughts kept drifting back to Quinn. She had used tough love to help plenty of her soldiers over the years, and their short-term annoyance had always washed right over her. Every one of them had flourished as a result. She knew she was doing the right thing, so why was she finding it so hard to do the same for Quinn?

CHAPTER FIFTEEN

Rolling up his sleeves, Quinn tilted his head to the sky. After a couple of days of rain, it was now so warm it felt like August. The weather was the one thing he hadn't been able to plan for, so he'd been relieved to wake up to a clear blue sky. Accepting a beer from Jiro, he clinked bottles.

"The garden looks amazing," Quinn said.

"Ellis and Carly are good at what they do," Jiro said.

"They've both been with you for a while?" Quinn tried to ignore the stab of jealousy at Ellis's name. The lad had been hanging around the office that Quinn and Abby shared too much for Quinn's comfort.

"Yes," Jiro said. "Lots of people love the job during the summer, but getting them to stay when the weather turns is a bit trickier. Carly and Ellis have been with us for two winters now."

Quinn chatted to the head gardener for a little longer before moving through the assembled groups, taking time to talk to each member of the team and their guests. He'd arranged the event as a kind of last hurrah before they were all too busy to take any holiday. He hadn't expected to enjoy himself as well, but he realised he was.

After spending the morning making sure everything was set up properly, his stress level had been through the roof. He'd found the cinema weekend hard work, but arranging this afternoon's party had shown him just how much Abby had carried on her shoulders without anyone else noticing.

A movement at the side of the house caught his eye, and he saw Abby walking in step with a man. At second glance, Quinn realised the man was Sam Harrison, the famous artist. Abby looked more relaxed than he had ever seen her, chatting and laughing. Something inside of Quinn clenched at the sight. Was she in a relationship with Sam? They were both carrying stacked boxes with the Honey & Rose Bakery logo neatly printed on them, and before Quinn could question the logic of his action, he strode over to them.

"I'll take those for you," he said, reaching out for the boxes Abby was carrying.

Her relaxed expression was almost instantly replaced with the blank look she seemed to deploy whenever she didn't want someone to know what she was thinking. Quinn knew he hadn't behaved very well over the last week, but her determination not to help him had hurt. She'd been his champion from the day he'd returned, but he hadn't realised just how much he'd come to rely on her support, or just how much she meant to him.

"It's fine," Abby said, taking a step back.

Quinn was vaguely aware of Sam Harrison's attention on him, but he couldn't take his eyes off Abby. He watched as strands of her hair danced around her face in the light breeze.

"If you don't mind taking these, I can go and get another load," Sam said, before turning to Abby. "You know if I don't, Tess will try to carry the rest on her own."

"Or Finn will try to eat them all," Abby said good-naturedly, her easy comfort with Sam making Quinn swallow.

Taking the boxes, he fell into step with Abby.

"So, you've decided to talk to me again?" she asked.

Quinn should have known she'd address his behaviour at some point. He knew he was behaving childishly, but despite the fact he felt faintly ridiculous, he couldn't quite let go of the hurt he still felt. "I have been talking to you," he said defensively.

"You know what I mean."

"I know it'll be a long summer if I don't find a way to forget that you turned your back on me," he said.

"Seriously?" Abby placed the boxes she'd been carrying on a table, turning to face him.

"You know I need to prove I can do this, that I need to change people's opinion of me here," Quinn said, putting his own stack of boxes down before gesturing around the garden.

"Yes, I do," Abby said, tucking her loose strands of hair behind her ears and briefly distracting Quinn from his frustrations.

"And you agreed to help me. We had a deal."

"We do," she replied, arms crossed.

"So why would you refuse to help me?"

"I have helped you."

"What is that supposed to mean?" Quinn crossed his own arms. "Have you been secretly organising things without telling me?"

As soon as the question was out, he wondered if that was exactly what she'd been doing. Everything had gone so smoothly.

"No," she said, her tone firm.

"Then what?"

"Look around," Abby said.

Quinn followed her gaze, taking in the barbecue station, the hula-themed bar, and the people spread out across the garden, talking and laughing. "What am I looking for?" he asked.

"Just this," Abby said, her head tilting towards the party. "You did this. You did it on your own. You didn't need any help."

Quinn frowned at her, wondering where she was going with this. After a moment, she rolled her eyes before walking away.

He watched her go, her words rattling through his brain. Walking to the bar, he asked for a bottle of beer and took a long drink.

Suddenly, with a blinding clarity, he realised exactly what Abby had done. He let his gaze travel again, taking in the happiness of the people around him. He'd made this happen on his own; the only thing that he couldn't claim credit for was the weather.

His gaze sought Abby; she'd known what he needed more than he had, and she'd found a way of giving that to him. His behaviour over the last week couldn't have been pleasant for her, but she'd taken the brunt of his frustrations in her determination to help him. He needed to talk to her.

Finally spotting Abby sitting on a blanket with Sam, Quinn hesitated, not sure if he wanted to face her with a boyfriend at her side. The sinking sensation that chain of thought created wasn't something he wanted to investigate, so he took another mouthful of beer and began to walk in Abby's direction.

"Cheers for today," Ellis called out to Quinn as he passed.

Smiling, but determined not to be derailed and risk losing his nerve, Quinn waved to the younger man and kept moving.

As he got closer, he noticed that Sam had his arm around a blonde woman. He wasn't Abby's boyfriend, then. He released a breath, something loosening inside him as his pace increased.

"Hello," he said, when he drew up beside the blanket Abby and her companions were sitting on. "Are you all having a nice time?"

"Yes, thank you," the blonde woman replied.

"These are my friends, Tess and Sam," Abby said with a smile that didn't quite reach her eyes. "They live in the village, and we have Tess to thank for the array of cupcakes."

"Ah, so you're the owner of the Honey and Rose Bakery?" Quinn said, smiling at the woman. Something about her seemed familiar.

"I am," she replied.

"Of course," Quinn said, clicking his fingers at her confirmation. "I think we met at the Christmas fair."

"We did. You were very gracious about me fobbing you off with all my leftovers," Tess laughed.

"I'm not going to complain. They were delicious."

"Thank you, although I don't know how you got Donna to agree to use the bakery for today when she makes incredible cakes of her own."

"I didn't give her a choice," Quinn explained. "I wanted to make sure the whole team here had the day off."

"I hope you're not too disappointed when you try my efforts!"

"If the way people are tucking into them is anything to go by, I'll be more than happy." Quinn gestured to a boy who was stuffing one into his mouth while holding another in his hand.

"Ah, that could be misleading," Tess said. "That's my son, Finn."

Quinn nodded. "My mother always said she had a devil of a time filling me up at that age." He turned to Sam and shook his hand. "Nice to meet you as well, Sam."

"Likewise," Sam said. "Why don't you join us for a bit?"

"I was actually hoping for a word with Abby, if you both don't mind me borrowing her for a few minutes?" Quinn asked, turning his attention back to Abby. She'd slid her sunglasses on, and he wished she hadn't because he really wanted to see her expression.

"I won't be long," Abby said, standing and gesturing for Quinn to lead the way.

His relief that she was prepared to speak to him after the way he'd behaved was short-lived, as he realised that he had to apologise to her now. Quinn wasn't used to apologising. Perhaps the fact that everyone had such low expectations of him meant that it was a challenge to disappoint them. He didn't think it would have been possible for him to let someone down until now.

Slipping through a gap in the hedge, Quinn entered the area that led through to the estate forest and waited for Abby to join him.

"I'm sorry," he began. "I have behaved childishly this week. I decided you weren't helping me, but you were."

Unable to take her lack of response, he began to pace.

"I get it now," he said. "I get that by making me do it on my own, you were proving to me that I am capable." He forced himself to look at her again. At the realisation that she was smiling, he took a deep breath, relief flooding him.

"I'm glad you see what I see," she said, the sun catching her red hair as she lifted her sunglasses onto the top of her head. Her smile lit up her features and turned an already pretty woman into someone extraordinarily beautiful.

"You think I'm capable," he said, holding her gaze.

"You are," she said with certainty.

When was the last time anyone had had such faith in him? When was the last time he'd had any faith in himself? Because of this woman, Quinn felt like he was worth something.

Without any conscious instruction from his brain, he closed the distance between them and cupped her face in his hands, lowering his head as he pressed his lips against hers. In that instant he felt transported, his entire world shrinking to the feel of Abby's mouth. Her hair was as silky as he'd dreamed. Tasting a hint of strawberry and feeling the soft warmth of her lips made him sigh. He reluctantly pulled back, knowing he'd overstepped.

"I'm sorry," he said, fighting the urge to pull her against his body. "I shouldn't have done that. I promise it won't happen again."

It looked as if apologising was going to become a habit around Abby. Summoning up the courage to look at her, he was disappointed to find her staring at the ground. She slid her sunglasses back on before looking up.

"It's okay," she said.

Quinn knew that Abby didn't have any interest in him beyond having a helper for the summer, but she had confidence in his abilities. He'd screwed that up by letting his hormones mistake her support for something very different.

"Shall we re-join the party?" Abby asked, turning and heading away before he could respond.

CHAPTER SIXTEEN

Throwing her running clothes on, Abby made her way from her bedroom to the kitchen area. Her head was pulsing. After Quinn had kissed her yesterday, she'd returned to Tess and Sam and started downing wine as fast as she could. Once the evening had arrived, Tess had joined her. Sam had read the mood and taken Finn home, leaving them to chat.

Abby wasn't someone who blurted out her feelings, and Tess wasn't someone who'd push her to. So, the pair had simply spent the evening drinking, reminiscing, and talking about nothing important.

Resting her head on the wooden cabinet door, Abby ignored the pleading look from Beatrice's dogs and found the energy to pour herself a glass of orange juice. Hopefully she could manage her morning run, which she knew from experience should make her feel normal again.

Taking a deep breath, she turned, startled at the sight of Quinn in the doorway, his jaw covered in dark scruff. His hair was dishevelled, and the shorts and T-shirt he was wearing were obviously pyjamas.

It was bad enough that she was finding him more attractive by the day, without having the torture of him kissing her yesterday. She'd helped enough young soldiers to know that a misplaced sense of gratitude could lead to them thinking they felt something more for her. It was normally easy enough to ignore until they came back to their senses. She was finding this an awful lot harder, though. She was well aware she could feel something for Quinn, if she let herself. But once his sense of gratitude wore off, where would that leave her?

"Morning," Quinn said, his tone far too chipper for her liking. "You're normally out much earlier than this."

"Morning," she said, concentrating on her glass of juice. At least the pulsing pain in her head was easing. "I had a lie-in." This wasn't true, but Abby wasn't about to admit that, even with the wine, she'd been unable to sleep much.

"It looked like you and Tess were having fun last night," Quinn said, something in his tone hitching, as though her answer really mattered to him.

"We did, but right now I wish we hadn't had quite so much fun." Abby was grateful that Quinn was avoiding the subject of their kiss. She hadn't been able to organise her thoughts, so she wasn't in any shape to be discussing it yet.

"You could probably skip the run for one day if you wanted to," Quinn suggested. "Even if that rabble want you to think otherwise."

She was up and back before Quinn was even out of bed most days, the dogs joining her. Despite her general fitness, she'd never be able to run enough to wear the trio out. The idea that Quinn knew her daily habits hadn't crossed Abby's mind, and the thought that he was so aware of her sent her a little further off kilter.

"Here." Quinn held out another carton of orange juice from the small fridge.

"Thanks," Abby said, taking it and refilling her glass. Forcing herself to drink, she ignored the urge to grimace. "Right," she continued, when she was able to speak without worrying that she'd throw up. "I'd better get going, or I'll be late starting work."

"Given the hours you put in, no one would begrudge you a late start whenever you wanted one," Quinn said.

His comment struck much deeper than Abby would have expected. She was surprised that anyone even noticed how hard she worked. Determined to put some space between herself and temptation, she made her way out of the kitchen. As she passed Quinn, the scent of his expensive cologne mingled with something else had her taking a deep breath in.

Abby mentally reprimanded herself as she headed for the back stairs. She'd already spent half the night obsessing over their kiss, and had given herself a thorough lecture on the stupidity of replaying something so brief. Thankfully, Quinn obviously didn't want to talk about it. He would probably be bitterly regretting his action soon enough, if he wasn't already. But she had no such luck; the kiss continued to fill her mind. She was just going to have to throw herself into work until she got a grip.

Having had a taste of being taken seriously and living up to expectations, Quinn realised he wanted more of that feeling. After getting through the day with a clearly hungover and exhausted Abby, he'd spent the evening locked in his room, putting together a proposal to share with Charlie the next day. After all, if he applied himself, surely he could be more valuable to his friend's business. Slipping into bed, he felt a sense of satisfaction.

Waking hours before his alarm was due to go off, his sense of anticipation stirring him from his sleep, Quinn decided to go and get a drink.

Walking down the hallway to the family kitchen, he tilted his head, soft sounds breaking the silence. After running the tap for a few seconds, he filled a glass and headed further down the corridor. The flickering of the ancient TV was visible in the darkened corridor.

Knowing the only other person currently staying on the family floor was Abby, Quinn continued until he reached the lounge doorway. Only the TV screen lit up the room and the battered furniture. It was a stark contrast to the luxurious and almost untouched stuff in the areas of Rose Hall that were open to the public. Quinn had always preferred it up here, where life felt a little more real and a lot less like an enormous display cabinet.

Abby was on the couch, her legs curled up at her side, her head resting on the arm. As he stepped into the room, Quinn realised she was sleeping. His mother's dogs were curled on the floor.

The sounds of the late-night travel show were interspersed with Abby's loud snores. Resisting the urge to laugh, Quinn lifted the blanket from the back of the couch and draped it over Abby.

"No," she muttered, making him freeze. "No, don't, it can't be." Her body shifted as she battled whatever was disrupting her sleep again.

Quinn wondered what plagued Abby's dreams. She often looked tired — beautiful, but tired. As she fell silent again, he finished covering her with the blanket and took a step back. Confident she was still sleeping, he turned to pick up his glass, intending to head back to his own room.

"NO," Abby almost shouted, making Quinn jump.

Startled, he turned back to see Abby sitting bolt upright, suddenly wide awake and looking very confused. The dogs were all peering up at her.

"What?" she asked, blinking.

Stepping towards Abby, Quinn dropped to his knees in front of her. "I think you were having a nightmare," he said, keeping his voice low, as though coaxing a nervous horse.

"I, um..." she started, clearing her throat. "I'm sorry if I disturbed you."

"You didn't. I couldn't sleep," Quinn said. He hesitated. "Do you want to talk about it?" He held her gaze as he spoke, silently willing her to trust him.

Eventually, Abby shook her head, and Quinn had to fight to keep his disappointment from showing.

"I'll head back to bed, then," he said, forcing his voice to sound light. "See you on Thursday." Rising to his feet, he padded back towards the doorway.

"Quinn..." Abby said.

His heart began to pound. Was she going to talk to him? Was she going to show that she didn't just see him as a mildly competent colleague? That she saw him as more than that?

"Thank you for the blanket," she said quietly.

"You're welcome," he said, his voice flat as he walked away.

CHAPTER SEVENTEEN

Having enjoyed a mid-afternoon cup of tea and a slice of cake outside, Abby was still trying to decide if she was pleased that her Quinn-free day had meant she didn't have to worry he'd raise the subject of their kiss, or if missing him had outweighed that benefit. Accepting that she wasn't going to find an answer today, she returned the dishes to Donna in the kitchen before heading back through the house. Just as she was about to re-enter the office, a voice called out to her.

"Miss Smith?"

Abby turned to see one of the older volunteers heading towards her. "Hello," she replied, smiling and desperately wishing she could remember the woman's name.

"There are a group of people in the entrance hall asking for you," the woman said. "They are being very loud."

"I'll go and see what's happening," Abby said, wondering who could be asking for her.

Ignoring the woman's muttering, she made her way straight to the entrance hall. She could hear the familiar, raucous voices before she entered, and a wave of hope washed through her.

"Smithy!" Burnett called as Abby approached. He had always been the loudest of the squad, so she wasn't surprised that he was the first to greet her.

"What are you lot doing here?"

"On our way to Dartmoor for an exercise. Since we know you work in a fancy place down this way, we thought we'd come and be annoying," Lasik said, elbowing Burnett out of the way to bundle Abby into a hug.

"I can't believe you're really here," Abby said breathlessly.

"Don't tell us, a few months in Civvy Street has addled your brain to the point where you can't see what's happening in front of you," Davies teased.

"My brain is as sharp as ever, thank you," Abby said, straightening her shoulders. "How long are you here?"

"We've booked into the pub in the village for the night, but we'll have to head off first thing," Chana said.

Abby smiled at her old corporal; the woman was a powerhouse of organisation and control, so Abby knew that every detail of the arrangements would be perfect. "That's great," she said. "I have a couple of hours before I can finish up for the day. Why don't you have a wander around and see just how fancy this place is, then we can head back to the village together?"

After completing her planned tasks for the day, Abby updated the list of things she and Quinn would have to complete tomorrow. He'd been incredibly apologetic about leaving her on her own today, but he'd had a prior commitment in London. She had enjoyed not having to concentrate on acting as though she didn't remember their kiss, but realising she'd actually missed him had been worse. Having her old friends and colleagues to distract her couldn't have been timed any better.

"Come on, then," she said, finding her old squad standing in the long hall, debating whether it was long enough to be a shooting range.

She let them head back to the minibus they'd arrived in and headed for her own car. She was definitely out of practice when it came to drinking large quantities of alcohol, and driving would give her the excuse not to try. The team would be merciless when she failed.

"What's your new sergeant like, then?" Abby asked.

"He's alright," Lasik said. "He can bench twice what you could."

Giving Lasik a good-natured swat, Abby rolled her eyes but let out a breath of relief. Part of the guilt that plagued her was due to the fact that her decision to leave meant the team would be stuck with a new sergeant, but Lasik's comment made it clear they approved of her replacement.

After ordering from the limited menu and making sure they all had drinks in front of them, Abby let herself relax and listen to updates about each of her old colleagues.

Taking a sip of her lime and soda, she took a quick inventory of everyone else's glasses. Judging the timing right to arrange a refill, she stood, making her way to the bar so she could order.

"Two more pints of lager, one large red wine, a double vodka and coke and two pints of cider, please," she said, smiling at the petite woman with cropped hair behind the bar.

"You look like you're all having fun," the woman said, smiling back as she started pouring the drinks.

"Are you Susie?" Abby asked.

The woman nodded.

"I'm Abby. I think we have a mutual friend, Tess."

"Oh, of course," Susie said. "You're working up at Rose Hall, aren't you?"

"Yes," Abby said, shoving her elbow back with as much force as she could manage as someone's hand slipped around her waist.

"Ouch," a voice protested.

Abby looked up at Lasik and raised her eyebrows.

"There was no need for that," he said.

"Are you telling me I really hurt you?" she asked, laughing.

"Well, no," he said, giving her a mock frown. "But most people don't elbow friends they haven't seen for months."

"True, but most friends would be smart enough not to try and sneak up on an ex-soldier fully trained in combat."

"Ah, but this friend wanted to make sure you hadn't lost your edge," he said, slinging his arm around her shoulders. "I thought you might need a hand carrying the drinks back."

Leaning into Lasik, Abby wrapped her arms around his waist, and let herself enjoy the sensation of feeling completely at home. "It's good to see you," she said, the words cracking slightly as she spoke.

CHAPTER EIGHTEEN

Pulling his car up outside the Angel Arms, Quinn rubbed his face and took a deep breath. He'd planned to stay in London overnight and head back to Rose Hall the next day, but he'd known that staying would be a bad idea. He'd been pictured in the gossip mags enough to know that going out drinking in a bad mood would only lead to more speculation about his lifestyle. And after he'd crashed and burned with Charlie, he hadn't been able to face sitting in his London flat with only his thoughts for company.

Quinn knew he was asking a lot of Charlie, hoping his old friend would see that he was able to do more than just offer his contacts up. He'd thought Charlie would jump at the chance for Quinn to do more work for him. He'd even offered to work on a commission-only basis to start with. He'd been so sure that Charlie would see the benefit of having another pair of hands. Instead, Charlie had actually laughed at him. The sound had seemed to follow Quinn all the way down the motorway. He knew Charlie hadn't meant to upset him, but one of your oldest friends telling you to be a good chap and stick to what you were good at had felt like a slap.

Letting his breath out slowly, Quinn decided he was going to get well and truly drunk. Going home to do that would be a lot more sensible than coming to the pub in Honeyford, where he'd more than likely have to walk three miles across the countryside to get home, and then do the same in the morning to pick his car up. Well, sensible or not, he was going to the pub. He couldn't face seeing Abby while he felt so utterly useless.

At the bar, he dredged a smile up for Susie. "Can I have a pint of Honeyford Pale, please?" he asked, naming the local brew.

"You look like you've had a rough day," she said, smiling to take the sting out of her words.

"It's not been one of my better ones," he said, glancing around as Susie poured his pint.

He noticed a huge man, the kind of man that looked as if he was pure muscle, settling in with a group of people he didn't know in the far corner. Turning back to the bar, something made him look around again, and he realised Abby was sitting with the group. The man was slipping in next to her and putting his arm around her shoulders.

The sight made his already tense stomach feel even worse. He really should have just gone home. Even his efforts at hiding from Abby had failed, and now on top of everything else, he had to accept that she was spoken for.

Pushing his hair back from his face, Quinn resigned himself to taking a few sips of his drink and slipping away before Abby realised he was here. At least that way he'd be able to drive home and drown his sorrows in the safety of his bedroom.

Taking a mouthful of his drink the moment Susie placed it in front of him, Quinn let out another sigh.

"That doesn't sound like you had a successful trip," Abby said, her soft voice warming him even as he flinched.

"It was fine," he said, knowing his tone and demeanour put the lie to his words.

"Are you meeting someone?" she asked.

"No," he said, as casually as he could. "I just fancied a quick one before heading home."

"Why don't you come over and join us?" she said. "Some of my old colleagues surprised me, and I'd love for you to meet them."

Old colleagues… The words reverberated for a moment, letting him hope his assumption had been wrong. Perhaps the muscular man was not her boyfriend. Quinn looked at her, trying to decide whether the offer was genuine.

"Please," Abby said, touching his arm. "It would mean a lot to me."

The warmth from her palm seeped through the thin fabric of his shirt. Abby never touched anyone. Quinn had realised that, as friendly as she was with people, she didn't seem to make the small gestures that were so familiar to him. The feel of her hand on his arm sent pure longing through him. He nodded and slipped off the bar stool as she led the way back to her friends.

"This is Lasik," Abby said, nodding at the big guy as he stood to allow her back into her original seat.

"Alright?" Lasik said, his hand almost swamping Quinn's as he gave a firm shake. As Lasik sat down, his arm settling back around Abby's shoulders, Quinn tried to focus on the rest of the introductions instead of the easy familiarity the pair had.

"Now, have you heard about the time Smithy here was running around in a sandstorm in only a towel?" Chana asked, waggling her eyebrows at Quinn.

"Oh God," Abby said. "You can't tell these stories when I'm sober."

"Well, get a drink then," Chana said with a shrug. "Because we're telling them."

"I have to drive back later," Abby said, her tone hopeful.

"I was planning on walking back if I can't get a taxi," Quinn said, suddenly wanting to hear all about Abby's military exploits.

"Fine," she said, fixing him with her gaze. "But this lot can put it away, so you have to promise you won't tell the boss if I can't get up for work tomorrow morning."

Quinn burst out laughing. He knew that whatever happened this evening, she'd be at work on time. With a smile he waved Susie over, slipping the money for the next round into her hand. Ignoring Abby's frown, he turned his attention to Chana.

"Now then, let's hear all about this towel," he said, his eyes wide as Abby groaned.

The rest of the evening had passed in a blur of laughter, but the lights and chatter of the pub were disappearing behind them as Quinn led the way through the darkness, and around the edge of one of the many maize-filled fields they would have to navigate on their way back to Rose Hall.

"Your friends are great," Quinn said, stumbling slightly as he turned to make sure the light of the torch on his phone was showing the way for Abby.

It was clear the group were bonded in a way that someone who hadn't served with them could never hope to be a part of. Yet they had managed to make Quinn feel included. He couldn't remember the last time he'd had so much fun. He was fortunate to have some great friends, but over the years their time together had become so serious. They were either out drinking and worrying about being on display, or they were having conversations that focused on what they were doing with their lives.

Abby's friends spent the whole time winding each other up. They teased and joked about things that could have been difficult and sensitive, but instead it brought everything out into the open and created a level of support and acceptance that Quinn envied.

"They can be a bit full-on if you aren't used to them, but yes, they are great," Abby said, and he could hear her smile in her voice.

"It was nice of them to come and see you." The fact that Lasik had simply given Abby a bear hug as they'd said their goodbyes had allowed Quinn to let go of the residual effects of his jealousy.

"I was so surprised," Abby said. "One of the tour guides came to find me. The way she told me there were people asking for me, you'd have thought a group of insurgents had abseiled into the entrance hall."

Quinn laughed at the image of one of the amazingly committed but slightly stuffy volunteers being presented with Abby's squaddie friends. They continued in silence for a few minutes.

"They are why I have nightmares," Abby said, the words quiet but making Quinn stop in his tracks.

He realised she had stopped a few steps behind him, her gaze on the ground. As he was trying to work out what to say, she started moving and passed him. He quickened his pace until he was by her side again.

"I keep seeing them hurt," she said. "I had to leave. I couldn't keep doing it, I couldn't keep losing people, but I feel so guilty."

Quinn took Abby's hand in his, and they came to a halt. This needed his full attention. "Why do you feel guilty?" he asked, careful to keep his tone neutral.

"Because I just left them. Me leaving won't stop them getting hurt."

"But you won't be responsible if it happens," he said.

Abby flinched at his words, her gaze meeting his. Eventually, she nodded.

Quinn lifted her hand, weaving their fingers together, hoping the gesture would show her that she had his support. Before he could think any better of it, he stepped closer. Keeping her hand in his, he used his other hand to cup her cheek. Pausing so she could step back if she didn't want this, he lowered his mouth to hers.

CHAPTER NINETEEN

For endless moments, all Abby could feel was Quinn's lips. The heat of his hand made her wish their bodies were pressed together.

As Quinn pulled back, resting his forehead on hers, Abby smiled. After his efforts to hide his jealousy of Lasik, she'd realised that Quinn was genuinely attracted to her. Lasik was a wall of solid muscle, and he knew just how good-looking he was, but they had only ever been friends.

The way Quinn had fit in with her squad had warmed Abby. Her civilian friends and military friends didn't usually mix very well, the former finding the latter too raucous, and the latter finding the former boring. Having at least a small part of the two sides of her life fit together so well had allowed her to fully feel like herself.

Walking in the dark with Quinn, a comfortable silence between them, the urge to share her nightmares with him had just built up until she had blurted the words out. Confiding in someone wasn't something she did very often. As soon as she'd spoken, the fear that he'd judge her had left her frozen, but his gentle tone had given her the courage to look at him. When she had, the sincerity and understanding in his gaze had knocked down yet more of her personal barriers.

"Wow," she said, finally voicing how his kisses made her feel.

"Indeed," he said huskily. "Would you mind if I did that again?"

Abby laughed. "I could probably cope if you did."

"Thank goodness," he said. "Because I've struggled to think about anything else since Monday."

"Me too," she said, a little thrill flowing through her at his admission.

Quinn pulled his hand away from hers and slipped it around her waist, his fingers flaring on her back as he pulled her closer, their bodies moulding to one another. The feel of his lean muscles made her moan softly.

The sound seemed to act as a catalyst, and Quinn deepened their kiss, his tongue exploring her own. Chest heaving, Abby reluctantly pulled back as his hand slipped under her blouse.

"Definitely wow," he said, pulling his hand back out and resting his forehead against hers again.

"We should get back," Abby said.

Quinn nodded. Holding hands, they completed the journey in comfortable silence. Once they had entered the family quarters at the top of Rose Hall, Quinn leant in, placing a gentle kiss on Abby's lips before stepping back.

"I'll see you in the morning," he said, his lip curling in that half smile that turned her insides to jelly.

Unable to speak, she nodded. He squeezed her hand gently before letting go and walking towards his own bedroom.

"Morning," Quinn said, holding a cup of tea out for Abby as she walked into their shared office the next day. "I thought you might need this."

"Thank you," she said. Feeling a shyness she hadn't expected, she smiled at him over the top of the cup as she took a sip.

"What jobs do you have for me today, then?" he asked.

"We need to get hold of History Alive to finish the plans for History Week," she said, the ground feeling more solid now she was focused on work. "If you don't mind catching up with Donna to see what information she needs so the kitchen can be prepared, that would be great. Then we can combine that with the requirements from the History Alive advisor and make sure we have all the information."

Donna and her team would have the unenviable task of stocking up and cooking to the requirements of the specialist historical advisor who was being sent by History Alive to ensure that the kitchen delivered authentic cuisine.

"No problem," Quinn said, heading for the door.

Abby turned slightly and let herself enjoy watching him leave, his trousers and shirt fitting him in a way that really wasn't designed to help her concentration. Switching on her computer, she took a large mouthful of tea before sinking into her chair and letting out a sigh.

"That's a big sigh." Tess's voice startled her.

"Tess, what are you doing here?" Abby asked, turning back to the door.

"What kind of welcome is that when I'm bringing you your favourite?" Tess laughed.

Abby's gaze immediately dropped to Tess's hands, the sight of a white Honey & Rose Bakery box making her smile. "Strawberry cheesecake?"

"Strawberry cheesecake," Tess confirmed. "And I'm here because Donna has booked me to make honey cakes for your History Week. I didn't think you'd forgive me if I came to the estate without seeing you." Tess sat next to Abby and poured herself a cup of tea.

"How are Sam and Finn doing?" Abby asked.

"They are great," Tess said, glowing. "Finn is on countdown to the summer holidays. Every day is just a relentless list of all the birds he hopes to see when he has time to be out in his hide."

"And how is Sam settling in?" Abby asked.

Tess and Sam had only started dating at Christmas, but it hadn't taken long for the celebrity artist to decide he was better off in Honeyford, with Tess and Finn, than in his London home.

"Great," Tess said. "I did worry Finn or I would find it strange having someone else in the house, or that Sam would struggle because … well, you know, but it's been brilliant."

Abby did know. Tess had bought her house with her husband, Mike. They had met and fallen in love young and would have still been together if Mike hadn't died. The reminder of the corporal who'd died under her command made Abby's stomach swoop. It wasn't as though she ever really forgot about him, or the other two soldiers she'd lost, but she usually managed to hold those thoughts at bay during the day.

"I bet Sam's made his mark," Abby said, wiggling her eyebrows at Tess in an attempt to lighten her own thoughts.

"He's been inspired, so he's actually been working into the early hours most nights recently." Tess blushed.

"Well, he has you as his muse."

"So, are you ready to tell me about Quinn?" Tess asked.

Glancing at the door, Abby frowned. "What do you mean?"

"Don't think I missed the fact that your entire mood changed after you went and had your private chat with him on Monday."

"So, you just came to see me so you could get the gossip?"

"You know me better than that," Tess said, holding her gaze. "I don't mind if you don't want to talk about it. I just want you to know that I'm always here for you if you need someone."

"Thank you," Abby said, her throat tightening. She paused. "We kissed."

"Okay..." Tess said, drawing the word out. "And how do you feel about that?"

How on earth was she going to express the swirling mess of emotions that surrounded kissing Quinn? "I don't know," she finally said.

Tess nodded. "Did you like it?"

"I think too much," Abby admitted, unable to meet Tess's gaze.

"Well..." Tess began, her tone suddenly changing mid-word. "Don't eat all that at once."

Abby's head jerked up. Quinn was standing in the doorway.

"Hello, Tess, this is a lovely surprise," Quinn said. "Donna said you'd been in to review plans with her, but I assumed you'd have gone by now."

"Hi, Quinn," Tess said. "I am just about to leave, but I wanted to invite Abby to dinner over the weekend." Turning to Abby, Tess raised her eyebrows in question.

"I'm not sure if I'll be able to," Abby said. "There will be lots of last-minute prep to do for next week."

"I'm sure we can spare you for one dinner," Quinn said gently, as though wanting to make it clear he wasn't trying to get rid of her.

"Can I let you know?" Abby asked. She knew Quinn meant well, but she also knew exactly why Tess had made the invitation, and she wasn't sure she was up for more conversation about what was happening just yet.

CHAPTER TWENTY

Quinn took a deep breath and looked across the room to where Abby was engrossed in work. It was two days since they had kissed, and she'd somehow managed to keep busy enough that he hadn't been able to raise the subject with her.

The fact they were sharing living quarters as well as an office meant that he was nervous about saying or doing anything that could make her feel uncomfortable, but now he was struggling to keep his focus purely professional.

"Abby," he said, drawing her attention to him.

She looked up and blinked a couple of times.

"Would you like to go for a walk when we're finished for the day?" he asked. He couldn't remember the last time he'd felt like this when asking a woman out. He was vaguely aware of the dogs raising their heads from their usual place under the table.

"That would be lovely," she replied, holding his gaze for a second longer before turning back to the files spread out in front of her.

The rest of the day passed so slowly that Quinn would have been checking the batteries in the grandfather clock, had he not known that Mr Heath ensured all the clocks were wound once a week without fail. Thankfully, it eventually passed five, and he pretended to be busy until Abby finally shut her own computer down.

"Still up for that walk?" he asked, keeping his tone carefully casual.

"Yes, I'll just nip for a wee first."

"I'll take the dogs and meet you out front."

Five minutes later, Quinn was pacing back and forth, the dogs watching him. He stopped when Abby appeared. Fortunately, Rose Hall closed at four during the week, so there hadn't been any staff loitering to see his discomfort.

The dogs instantly made their way towards her, and the smile she gave him made him want to take her face in his hands and kiss her again.

They walked in silence, heading towards the paths that led through the estate's woodlands.

"I want you to be happy here, and I'm sorry if I made you uncomfortable on Wednesday night," Quinn said, the words spilling out the second they were out of sight of the house.

"Do you mean because of the kiss?" Abby asked.

He nodded. "I don't want you to feel like you didn't have a choice, or like you owe me anything because we are both working and living here."

Abby was silent for a moment before she replied. "Do you think I would have kissed you if I hadn't wanted to? Do you think you could have kissed me if I hadn't wanted you to?"

Quinn's head snapped up. "Um, I don't know," he said.

"Quinn, I'm a trained and experienced soldier. If I hadn't wanted that kiss, or the one on Monday, they wouldn't have happened. I'm more concerned that you are mistaking gratitude for attraction."

Quinn frowned at that; was Abby saying she was only kissing him out of gratitude? Gratitude for what?

"I've had enough new squaddies mistake their gratitude towards me for something else to know that it's quite common," she said.

After a few minutes, the pieces finally fell into place. "So, you are worried that I only kissed you because I appreciate you helping me?" Quinn asked.

"Yes," Abby said, stopping but not turning to face him.

Quinn moved so he was in front of her, but with enough distance between them so that he wasn't crowding her. "So, if I'm understanding this right, I have been holding back because I was worried I would make you feel uncomfortable, and you've been holding back because you thought I'd only kissed you out of some sense of gratitude."

"It looks like it," Abby replied.

"I want to make it very clear that, while I appreciate your help, my desire to kiss you has nothing to do with me being grateful. But given that we live and work together, does that make you feel awkward or uncomfortable?"

Abby shook her head. "Not at all. I've spent the last decade in the military. If living and working with someone was an issue, I'd have been single for a very long time."

The thought of her dating other people sent a white-hot pain through him, but Quinn shoved it away. Given his lifestyle over the last few years, his jealousy over her past was entirely irrational. "Can I kiss you again?" he asked.

"How about I kiss you?" she suggested, closing the distance between them.

CHAPTER TWENTY-ONE

Abby lifted her arms and pulled Quinn's head down. When their lips met, his entire body seemed to sigh with relief.

The kiss was hot and needy, and as his lips moved down her neck, he let out a moan that told her he was enjoying this just as much as she was. As he reached her collar, he laughed.

"Damn it," he said, lifting his head and resting his forehead against hers. "Foiled by your blouse."

Despite herself, Abby stiffened; she had enough criticism of her choice of outfits from her mother.

"You have no idea how these blouses have driven me insane over the last few weeks," Quinn said, his voice rough.

"How can they possibly do that? I wear them buttoned up to my throat." Abby's words slammed home the memory of what he'd find when those buttons were undone; she might talk a good talk about liking the military style of dress, but that was only part of the story.

Quinn's gaze met hers as he traced a finger around her collar. Her breath hitched at the sensation, her muddled mind trying to work out whether he'd have felt the ragged edge of her scars.

"I have spent more time than I'd like to admit imagining just what you look like underneath all that fabric," Quinn murmured. "You know that blue blouse you have, the really bright one? When you move, it clings to every line of your body. I haven't been able to stop thinking about stripping you out of it." His voice cracked, revealing how hard he was controlling himself right now.

Abby's lips parted, her chest lifting, and she pulled him back to her, the movement harsh as her lips slammed into his again. Suddenly, all thoughts of her scars were gone, thrown out of her mind by the overwhelming need to touch him, to be touched. Her hands slid around his waist, tugging at his shirt in her haste to feel his skin. The sensation of his muscles seeming to jump under her touch fuelled her need even further. The sensation of his strong hands roaming her body made her push against him more firmly.

One palm brushed her ribs and the underside of her breasts; the other slid lower and grasped her buttocks. His groan of need flared through her, her own answering as she attempted to get even closer. This wasn't like the gentle kisses and hesitant touches of before. This was hungry and desperate, and Abby didn't think she'd ever be able to get enough of him. The sound of the dogs whining slowly filtered through and, staggering slightly, they pulled apart and laughed.

"Shall we take this inside?" Quinn mumbled, his mouth still pressed against her lips as he spoke.

Her breath coming in short bursts, Abby nodded, not sure she could trust her voice.

Quinn lifted her hand, twining his fingers through hers, and led them back to the house. The dogs, seemingly confused at having their walk cut short, whined for a moment before following them.

Abby and Quinn almost ran through the side door that remained unlocked until the very last of the staff had left. Without any concern over who might see them, Quinn kept up the urgent pace along the winding corridors of the ground floor and up the stairs to the first floor, not slowing until they reached the family quarters. The dogs bounded off to the TV room.

As the door swung behind them, Quinn backed Abby against the wall of the corridor, his mouth crashing against hers. Abby was a trained soldier, used to command and control, but the way Quinn devoured her lips, her neck, every inch of skin he could reach, made her realise just how much she liked it when someone lost control with her, and made her lose control herself.

"Could we go to my room?" Quinn asked, and Abby nodded. Leading them to his bed, Quinn stood motionless, as though suddenly nervous. "Are you sure?"

"I have never been more sure of anything," Abby said, undoing his shirt and slipping it off his shoulders. Being able to run her hands over his broad shoulders and down his chest was a thrill like no other, and watching his muscles twitch as she did so gave her a feeling of power she had never experienced.

Backing onto Quinn's bed and scooting along until her head lay on his pillow, she watched him, enjoying the way his eyes widened, his chest rising and falling with his rapid breathing, his eyes unblinking as he watched her. Finally, and far too slowly for her liking, Quinn moved, inching along the bed until he was finally level with her.

"You're in my bed," he said, the words hitching with his intensity.

Before Abby could respond, Quinn pushed himself up on his elbow, leaning over her as his fingers grazed her lips, then traced over her chin. As he opened the top button of her blouse, she leant back, part of her wondering if she should warn him, but the other part was determined not to sabotage this. She had been a soldier for a long time; you didn't get through that unscathed. She wouldn't let her own insecurities ruin this. Still, she closed her eyes, unable to bring herself to see the expression on his face when he saw the mess that was her shoulder for the first time.

Even with her eyes closed, the moment he registered her scars was obvious. His movements stilled completely, his voice rough as he spoke.

"What happened?"

"Shrapnel," she said, her voice cold, controlled, determined not to let any glint of vulnerability show.

Quinn was still and silent for so long that she wondered if he would pull back, but then, so gently she wondered if she was imagining it, his lips began to trace the edges of her scarring. "You were worried?" he asked, his surprise clear.

She gave a small shrug. "It's not exactly attractive," she said quietly.

Lifting himself up, he curled his hand around her shoulder. "You survived," he said. "All that matters is that you survived. Your scars are a part of you, a part of who you are, and because of that, they simply make you more beautiful."

Unable to articulate the way his statement made her feel, Abby pulled Quinn's head down to hers and pressed her lips to his, needing to lose herself in his body, in him.

Stirring, Abby blinked, the room swimming into focus as her memories of the previous night flooded her. The feel of an arm around her and the warm muscle heating her back let her know that Quinn was still with her.

"Good morning," he said, and she turned in his arm, wanting to see him.

"Morning," she said.

He eased closer, his arms tightening as he placed a kiss on her forehead.

"What time is it?" she asked.

"Just after six," he said, his voice deep and scratchy from sleep.

"What?"

"I know, it's stupidly early."

"I never sleep this long," she said, trying to work out what time they had finally fallen asleep last night. Enjoying the feel of Quinn's hand stroking up and down her back, she let her eyes flutter closed. Then a loud rumble from her stomach made them both laugh.

"I guess that puts paid to us spending the rest of the morning here," Quinn said.

"Well, you did deprive me of dinner last night," Abby said, raising her eyebrow.

"I didn't hear any complaints at the time."

"Well, I was a little distracted."

"Let me hop in the shower quickly, then I'll make it up to you." Quinn placed a gentle kiss on her lips, before pulling back and climbing out of bed. "Don't go anywhere. I like having you in my private space."

Abby watched the twitch of his muscles as he walked across the room, enjoying the fact that he was entirely comfortable walking around naked. She laughed as his off-key singing echoed from the en-suite.

Climbing out of bed, she walked to the bathroom and watched as he lathered his hair with shampoo. Once he'd rinsed it out, he caught sight of her standing there and slid the glass panel back.

"I thought you were more of a participant than spectator," he said, holding his hand out in invitation.

"I was just admiring your singing skills," she said.

"Yes, I know, I'm terrible. But I can't seem to stop myself this morning."

At that, Abby strode forward. Sliding one hand up his soapy chest, she used her other hand to pull the glass door closed behind her.

Sitting at the chipped Formica table, Abby frowned as Quinn fussed around her, offering more toast and tea.

"I'm fine," she said. "Why don't you sit down and enjoy your own breakfast?"

Quinn sank into the chair opposite her, still avoiding eye contact.

"What's the matter?" Abby asked, determined not to slip into silent worrying about whether he regretted last night, or this morning.

"Well, I, um…" he started, and she resisted the urge to tell him to spit it out. "How do you want to handle this with the rest of the team?"

"What do you mean?"

"Well, do you want them to know about this — about you and me? That we're together?"

Abby's entire body seemed to let out a sigh, the tension draining away. The fact that she was leaving at the end of the summer, and that he'd likely be leaving as well, wasn't important right now. She wanted this for as long as they were both here. "Are you embarrassed about us?" she asked.

His head snapped up. "God, no. If anything, I thought you might be. It's not so unrealistic to think that you might not like the idea of people knowing you're sleeping with the screw-up heir to this place. Especially given my reputation."

"I'm not even going to start unpicking the amount of rubbish in that statement," Abby said. "Why don't we just see how it goes? We don't have to do some big announcement, but we don't need to keep it secret either. What happens between us is no one's business but our own."

CHAPTER TWENTY-TWO

Scooping the last of the scrambled egg into his mouth, Quinn groaned with satisfaction. It had been a week since he'd somehow managed to convince Abby to join him in his bed, and he was enjoying the fact she'd been there every night since. He just couldn't get enough of her. They hadn't exactly told anyone, but he had a suspicion that at least Donna was aware of how close he and Abby had become. After all, he couldn't imagine any other reason why she had insisted on sending a treat breakfast up to them both.

"Are you sure there isn't any more?" Quinn asked.

"Afraid so," Abby said, her own plate still holding a small amount of the delicious breakfast.

"Perhaps you'd like to share?" Quinn raised his eyebrows with mock hope. He knew full well that Abby's appetite matched his own, but it didn't hurt to try. This quiet time in the morning was rapidly becoming one of his favourite times of the day. It was just him and Abby together, enjoying the simple routine of preparing for the day ahead.

Abby just gave him a look, before scooping the last of the meal up.

"Fine, I'll just have to make do with more coffee," Quinn said, turning his attention to the enormous pot.

The sound of Abby's phone ringing interrupted their good-natured back and forth. Her expression shifted to delight as she took in the caller ID and answered. "Rob, how lovely!"

Quinn stood and began washing up. The sound of Abby peppering her brother with questions about his wife and twin daughters made him smile, but not as much as hearing her say how much she was enjoying her time at Rose Hall. He quietly hummed to himself, so as to give Abby some semblance of privacy.

"Do you mean Quinn?" Abby asked, the sound of his name drawing Quinn's attention back to her conversation. "He did not escape rehab to hide out here," she continued, her tone surprisingly sharp. "Honestly, Rob, I promise it's fine. He's a really great guy."

The sound of Abby defending him made Quinn's chest expand. She clearly didn't believe a word of what she was hearing. He had never had a drugs problem, and he'd certainly never been to rehab.

As Abby wound up her call with her brother, Quinn swallowed hard. "We should probably talk about the press coverage I get," he said, pushing his hair back.

"We don't need to talk about anything," Abby said firmly. "I've worked with people who've had drugs problems, and I've worked with recovering addicts. You are clearly neither of those things."

"I've never had a problem with drugs, but I have wasted a lot of time partying. A lot of the coverage is true."

"Quinn," Abby said, standing and walking over to him. "Everyone has a past. That doesn't have to define their future. I haven't been living under a rock; I know you have a reputation for dating lots of women, and for liking a party and a drink. All I ask is that you be honest with me. I don't know what this thing between us is, and I don't think we need to define it just now. All we need to do is be open with each other."

"I can do that," Quinn said, finally looking up to meet her gaze.

"And," she added, the confidence in her tone slipping slightly, "for as long as this lasts, I don't want to have to worry about other women."

Raising his free hand, Quinn smoothed a stray hair back from Abby's face, before cupping her cheek in his palm. "I promise you, there is only you," he said, his words ringing with an intensity that he hadn't expected. But the moment they were out, he realised just how much he meant them.

Abby opened her mouth to respond but was interrupted by a male voice in the hall shouting, "Knock, knock!"

Stepping back and letting Quinn's hand go, Abby stuck her head into the hallway. "Ellis!" she said. "What are you doing up here?"

"I said to Donna I'd come and bring the breakfast dishes down for her," Ellis said. "How have you two managed to wangle a full fry-up?"

If Quinn hadn't been wrestling with a level of jealousy and insecurity he should have been old enough to master, he wouldn't have crossed the room and stood just out of sight, so he could hear the conversation. Unfortunately, despite the wonderful week he'd had with Abby, he couldn't shake his fears, especially given the way the younger man seemed to hang around Abby.

"I had something I wanted to talk to you about privately," Ellis said, his tone nervous in a way that Quinn didn't like.

"What about?" Abby asked.

"Um, well," Ellis began awkwardly. "It's about Lisa. I really like her, but I don't know how to tell her. I was hoping you could help me."

Quinn let out a breath and took a step backwards, thinking that the younger man didn't need him listening in on this conversation. He felt a sympathy for Ellis that would have been impossible when he'd thought he was a rival for Abby's attentions. The thought made him pause. Perhaps that was what was behind Lisa's comments about Abby. If Lisa thought Ellis's head had turned in Abby's direction, it would explain why the younger woman had been so harsh. Despite what Abby thought, the majority of the team really liked her.

Smiling, Quinn realised that if Ellis asked Lisa out, then his part in the pact he and Abby had made would be done. She had never really needed his help.

CHAPTER TWENTY-THREE

"Here," Abby said, approaching the historical costumier, Theresa, with an armful of discarded Elizabethan and Jacobean jerkins. "These were over by the armoury."

Theresa laughed as she scooped the pile out of Abby's hands. "That's pretty normal for these events. The kids find me first, get dressed up, and then get super excited when they find the armoury."

"I guess beautiful fabric can't really compete with the chance to dress up like a knight heading for battle when you're a child," Abby said.

They were four days into History Week at Rose Hall, and she was loving every moment of it. The event had been timed to coincide with the start of the school summer holidays, and the stream of visitors had kept everyone busy.

"Will you let me provide you with an outfit for the dinner tonight?" Theresa asked.

"Oh, I don't need one," Abby said. "The serving staff already have their own costumes, and I'll just be there in the background in case anything goes wrong."

"But Mr Beaumont has agreed to wear a costume so he can greet the guests as they arrive," Theresa said.

As though called by the sound of his name, Quinn stepped up behind Abby, gently placing his hand on the small of her back.

Unable to stop herself, she turned and smiled at him. The last couple of weeks had passed in a flurry of work, but little touches and glances had connected them, and the nights spent together had built a sense of togetherness that Abby couldn't remember experiencing before. The fact she was even sleeping better meant she felt energised, and it was taking far less effort to get through the events. She was still having nightmares, but they were less frequent, and waking in Quinn's arms seemed to stem the building panic and guilt. Part of her knew she should worry about that; she couldn't afford to get reliant on him, but she was enjoying feeling properly rested too much to let it stop her for now. As with their relationship, she was just going to enjoy it while it lasted.

"You're dressing up for the dinner?" Abby asked Quinn, the idea of him dressed in stockings and those knee-length trousers making her laugh.

"Just you wait," he said, waggling his eyebrows.

"Okay," Abby said, turning to Theresa when she finally had control of her amusement. "I'm game, as long as I can move in whatever you choose for me."

That evening, the first of three consecutive history dinners, Abby stood in one of the less used offices. Theresa had set out a full-length mirror next to a selection of clothing.

"I don't have to wear what passed for underwear in the 1600s, do I?" Abby asked.

"No," Theresa said. "It doesn't go down well with the traditionalists, but I've always subscribed to the idea that it's only what you see on the surface that matters."

"Do people really do the whole thing?" Abby asked.

"You'd be surprised," Theresa said, indicating for Abby to strip out of her suit. "Discussions can get very heated when you're dealing with re-enactors."

Standing in her underwear, Abby studied the pile of dresses as Theresa lifted them one at a time and discarded them just as quickly. Finally, she settled on a black dress that was threaded through with silver and gold. As she helped Abby step into the hooped skirt, her gaze caught her scars, but she didn't comment. She then picked up a thin pillow.

"What is that?" Abby asked.

"It's a bum roll. We'll tie it around your waist, and it'll give you shape at the back of the dress."

"No, I'm drawing the line at that one. This will be plenty," Abby laughed.

"Now, given that you don't want to wear a bum roll, I assume you won't want us to put your hair up with a wire frame to give it more volume," Theresa said, "so we should let it down." She tugged out the band holding Abby's standard bun in place.

Just then, Lisa opened the door and peered in. "Wow," she said. "You look amazing."

"Um, thanks," Abby said uncertainly.

"You have such beautiful costumes," Lisa said, turning her attention to Theresa for a moment before looking back at Abby. "I just wanted to let you know the first guests will start arriving in about fifteen minutes. Are you okay for me to head off? Ellis is taking me out."

"Thank you, Lisa," Abby said. "And yes, head off and enjoy your evening."

Lisa nodded, beaming in a way that only young love could inspire. Abby hadn't really given Ellis any advice other than to talk to Lisa, but it was clear the young man had taken her literally and done just that. Abby was a little embarrassed that Quinn had had to point out the likely source of Lisa's previous negativity towards her, but she was pleased that her relationship with the young woman had improved.

Theresa placed her hands on Abby's shoulders and turned her to face the full-length mirror. "What do you think?" she asked.

"It's a beautiful dress," Abby said, tracing one of the threads of silver with her finger. "Thank you so much for letting me borrow it."

"Wait until that man of yours sees you." Theresa winked. "You can thank me after that."

Abby stilled; they might not be hiding it, but it was the first time anyone had commented on her relationship with Quinn. "Is it that obvious?"

"I'm old enough to be able to recognise young love," Theresa said with a shrug.

Abby stared at her. "We're not in love," she said, her words firm as she ignored the swell of panic that seemed to be trying to force its way out of her corset.

"My husband has been gone for a few years now," Theresa said, "but I still remember what love looks like."

"I'm sorry," Abby said, deciding this wasn't the time to argue with the woman, and hoping the sincerity of her words came through.

"Don't be. We had a lot of wonderful years together," Theresa said with a wistful smile that made Abby's panic subside a little. Perhaps it would be possible for her to remember Quinn with such warmth when the summer was over.

Standing in the hallway, Quinn smiled as a steady flow of guests arrived for the evening. He suspected it was going to feel like another very long night, but he couldn't help but smile at the enthusiasm of the arrivals. When Theresa had offered to loan him an outfit, he had jumped at the chance. He couldn't remember the last time he'd worn fancy dress, and much to his surprise, he was enjoying his role as host for the evening. The high spirits of everyone who'd arrived so far had buoyed his own good mood. The only thing that would improve his evening would be Abby's company.

As if conjured by his thoughts, Abby appeared, slipping through a side door and into the entrance hall. She was wearing a long, full dress that seemed to sparkle as she moved. Her dark red hair was down, waves of it brushing the tops of her shoulders, framing her pale face and seeming to highlight her natural beauty.

As Abby caught sight of Quinn, her eyes widened, and she seemed to swallow as her gaze travelled down his body and back up. If it hadn't been for the raw need that seemed to radiate from her, he'd have felt self-conscious. As it was, he wondered just how long it would be before he could get her upstairs.

As she approached, he resisted the urge to laugh. Every third step, she dropped the pile of fabric she'd hooked over her arms and had to gather it up again before attempting to walk further.

"Not a word," she said.

"Not a fan of dresses, then?" he asked.

"Dresses are fine," she said. "Whatever this thing that's masquerading as a dress is, not so much."

"You look lovely," Quinn said, slipping his hand around her waist as she neared. Leaning down, he placed a gentle kiss on her lips, pulling back before he could forget where he was and what they were supposed to be doing.

As they welcomed the next few arrivals together, Quinn realised that this was all he wanted: Abby by his side. No matter what he was doing, her presence made it even better.

He might not know what he wanted to do with his life, but he had a feeling that it wouldn't matter what it was, as long as she was with him.

The sound of his phone ringing pulled his attention from the group of women who had arrived, dressed in an array of costumes that were clearly homemade.

"It's Mother," Quinn said, smiling at Abby. "I won't be long." Taking a few steps back, he hit answer and smiled as his mother's face filled the screen.

"Quinn," she said, "I'm a grandmother." Her excitement seemed to radiate through the phone.

"Wow, Cordelia had the baby?" Quinn asked.

"Yes, a baby girl," Beatrice said, beaming.

"How's Cordelia?"

"She's wonderful. Would you like to see your niece?" She started moving before he could answer, and he realised that she was in the hospital.

"I'd love to," Quinn said, thrilled that despite the miles between them all, he was getting the opportunity to be a part of such an important family moment.

"Cordelia, say hello to your brother."

"How are you?" Quinn asked as soon as Cordelia's face appeared on his screen.

"I'm good," she said, and he took in her flattened hair and shiny face. She didn't look her usual polished self, but there was no denying the absolute happiness that shone from her features.

"So where is the girl of the hour?" Quinn asked.

The phone tilted, and he could see the tiny face, scrunched up, skin pink and mottled, tucked into Cordelia's arm. His heart seemed to swell, his eyes prickling, as he took in his niece.

"Mia, meet your Uncle Quinn."

"She's beautiful," Quinn said. "Did it all go okay?"

"Yes, it was easy enough. Everyone at the hospital was marvellous," Cordelia said.

"Ignore her," Noah, her husband, said. His face appeared in the corner of the screen. "It was the scariest thing I've ever seen. Your sister was incredible."

Quinn smiled at the obvious adoration between Cordelia and her husband. After chatting for a few more minutes, he said his goodbyes, leaving Cordelia to rest.

"Everything okay?" Abby asked, when Quinn made his way back to her side.

He nodded, not quite in control of his emotions.

Abby gave him a gentle smile. As always, she seemed to understand just what he needed. She didn't ask any more and simply slipped her hand into his, giving it a small squeeze as she turned her attention back to the newest group of arrivals.

CHAPTER TWENTY-FOUR

"What will you do after the summer?" Donna asked, topping Abby's glass up.

Quinn grew still, his own glass halfway to his mouth before he forced himself to take a sip. He needed to ensure that the importance of her response wasn't completely obvious to everyone around them. The Sunday evening tradition of finishing up the opened champagne bottles had quickly become one of Quinn's favourite parts of the week. It felt special to join in with the rest of the team here.

"I don't know yet," Abby said, giving a shrug.

"Maybe Beatrice will ask you to stay on," Lisa said, smiling broadly, her hand firmly in Ellis's. "You've been doing an amazing job."

"I'm used to moving around a lot," Abby said. "I'm not sure I'm ready to settle in one place just yet."

Quinn froze. The conversation moved on, and the chatter continued to surround him, but he couldn't stop Abby's words from swirling around his head. It was entirely possible she had simply found a response that was designed to make sure people didn't feel sorry for her if she had to leave at the end of the summer, but he didn't think that was the case. They hadn't had a single conversation about the future, but he'd begun to believe that whatever came next, they would be together. To hear Abby make it clear that wasn't necessarily the case was like getting punched in the stomach. Swallowing the rest of his drink in one go, he held his glass out for a refill, determinedly ignoring the sideways glances around him.

Giving Lisa a kiss, Ellis turned his attention to Abby. "Ready to go, Abby?" he asked.

Quinn knew Abby was going to stay at her friend Tess's for the night, but he hadn't realised that she was getting a lift with Ellis.

"Yes. Thanks, Donna," Abby said, placing her glass in one of the dishwashers before moving to follow Ellis.

The sight of the younger man smiling at her as he waited made something inside Quinn snap. Without giving himself time to second-guess his actions, he put his own glass down and followed.

Once in the corridor, he called out, "Abby, could I have a minute before you go?"

Abby and Ellis turned.

"I'll meet you at my car," Ellis said, addressing Abby.

"Thanks, Ellis. I won't be long," she replied. She faced Quinn. "What's up?"

"I'll miss you tonight," he said, the words he really wanted to say failing him. Closing the distance between them, he brushed the back of his fingers down her cheek.

"I'll miss you too," Abby said, her expression serious.

"I hope you have a great time with Tess tonight," he said. "Tell her I say hello."

"I will," Abby said, leaning into him. Placing a gentle kiss on his lips, Abby frowned. "I really am going to miss you tonight."

"You say that like it's a bad thing," Quinn replied, forcing a teasing lilt into his tone. "But don't they say that absence makes the heart grow fonder?"

Abby opened her mouth but closed it again without speaking. Quinn's heart pounded in response. What had she been going to say?

Before he could ask, she placed another gentle kiss on his lips and turned, walking towards the exit. Suddenly, he couldn't breathe. It was as though he was watching her walk away from him for good. "Abby!" he shouted, just before she turned the corner. "Did you mean what you said about not settling anywhere?" Suddenly, he was unable to continue without knowing.

Her gaze dropped to the floor again. "I'll see you in the morning," she said, her words quiet. The way her eyes firmly avoided his made it clear she knew exactly what he was really asking. She turned on her heel and walked out of sight.

Taking a deep breath, Quinn stood frozen in place, unable to do anything other than stare at the spot where Abby had disappeared from view.

For the first time in his life, he'd started to feel he had found his place. If Abby wouldn't be at Rose Hall with him, at his side, would he actually want to be here? He had a feeling he wouldn't. What he really wanted was to be wherever she was, but her lack of response made him realise that the sentiment was entirely one-sided.

Knowing he should go back to the kitchen to quell any gossip he'd created by following Abby, Quinn headed in the opposite direction. It wasn't as if the staff hadn't already worked out that he and Abby were more than colleagues, and he couldn't face anyone else right now.

Heading towards the family quarters, Quinn realised that even his own bedroom wouldn't give him any respite from thinking about Abby. They'd spent every night wrapped up in each other for the last few weeks. Now he felt adrift in a way he hadn't ever experienced.

CHAPTER TWENTY-FIVE

"Come on through," Tess's warm voice called as Abby knocked on her door.

Letting herself in, Abby walked through to Tess's kitchen.

"Sorry, I'll be with you in a moment," Tess said, her tone harassed. "Please give me my slipper back, Biscuit." She was addressing her beagle, who finally gave up the slipper so it could come and sniff Abby.

"Hi, Abby," Tess said. "Would you mind helping me carry some stuff out to the garden?"

"No problem," she said, bending to give the dog a rub behind her ears before turning back to help Tess.

"Thanks, I should be more prepared by now, but I had to run some cakes over to the retirement community and it's put me behind," said Tess. "Finn and Sam should be back soon. We'll eat when they get home, if that's okay?"

"Perfect," Abby said. Tess was notorious for overloading her schedule with her desire to do everything for everyone. "Where are they?"

"In the woods, birdwatching," she said. "They went a few hours ago, so I don't imagine they'll be long now."

Loading trays with napkins, plates, cutlery, and an immense array of condiments, Tess indicated for Abby to take one and led the way into the back garden.

"Wow," Abby said. Glancing around, she took in the beautiful garden. A trellis covered in pale pink blooms framed one side of a huge wooden table surrounded by chairs, clearly a space for friends and family.

It had been a couple of years since Abby had been to the house that Tess had once shared with Mike. He'd been Abby's corporal, her right hand, until he'd died during a tour of duty with her. Blinking at the thought of how much Mike would have loved this wonderful space, Abby plastered a smile on her face and forced herself to keep walking. Only her full hands prevented her from reaching up and touching her scars.

"Are you thinking about Mike?" Tess asked astutely.

Not wanting to bring up difficult memories for Tess, but not wanting to lie either, Abby swallowed, busying herself with taking things off the tray she had been carrying.

"It's okay," Tess said, her voice gentle. "I still think about him all the time."

Abby looked up. "How do you do it?" she asked, the question spilling out before she could stop it.

"I will always love Mike," Tess said. "But I've finally accepted that having a life now doesn't diminish that in any way."

Unable to hold her gaze, Abby turned her attention back to the table. "I wasn't judging," she said quietly.

"I know you weren't," Tess said. "But are you judging yourself?"

Abby's head swung round, her gaze meeting Tess's.

"I hope you know that everyone wants you to be happy too?" Tess said. "Leaving the military doesn't mean that you have to stop living."

Abby's mouth dropped open as she floundered around for something to say. Was that what she was doing? Was guilt making her put her life on hold?

"Mum!" Finn's voice broke the silence. As he appeared around the side of the house, he spotted Abby and ran over, giving her a huge hug. "Aunty Abby!"

Wrapping her arms around him, she laughed. "Hiya, Finn," she said. "Did you see any cool birds today?"

Giving Sam a wave hello, Abby let Finn lead her over to the table and sat next to him, so he could show her his notes from his day of birdwatching. Glancing over to Sam and Tess, Abby smiled at the sight of Sam pulling Tess into his arms and kissing her. The easy comfort the pair had with each other clearly didn't diminish their passion.

Turning her attention back to Finn, Abby rubbed her chest. She was fine, she didn't need that. She knew she wasn't designed to settle down, so there was no reason for this squeeze of pain.

By the time Finn had finished talking, Tess and Sam had brought out a range of mouth-watering dishes.

"It's too warm to cook today," Tess said, sinking into the chair opposite Abby. "I hope cold meats and salads are okay."

"This looks amazing," Abby said. Helping herself to a selection of the salads and pasta dishes, she added a couple of slices of carved chicken.

"So, how is it going at Rose Hall?" Sam asked, filling his own plate.

Abby blinked, not responding until she was certain his question was one of innocent interest. "It's great," she said. "The team there are really friendly and very experienced."

"Wow," Tess said, her tone teasing. "They must be exceptionally well organised if *you* think they're good."

Abby realised that she'd stopped seeing the time the team at Rose Hall spent on chatter and cups of tea as frivolous. She now understood how important that was for them to maintain the connection they all had with each other. She briefly wondered when her perception had shifted before Tess asked the awkward question.

"How are things with Quinn?"

"Fine," Abby said, knowing her effort to keep her tone light hadn't quite worked. "What about you, Finn, how are you enjoying the school holidays?"

Keeping her gaze on Finn, Abby waited to see if she'd get away with the clunky subject change. When Tess let Finn chatter away about his plans for the autumn term, when he would be in the last year of primary school, Abby let out a sigh of relief.

The rest of the meal passed in friendly chatter, and Abby relaxed into the evening.

"Come on, you," Sam said to Finn. "Time for us to clear up."

"Do I have to?" Finn asked, his tone edging towards a whine.

"Yes," Sam said firmly. "And you know why."

"Because when someone takes the time to make us a nice dinner, it's not fair to expect them to clear it up as well," Finn said, his voice taking the tone of someone who'd heard the same thing countless times.

"Exactly," Sam said, ruffling his hair. "Well done, lad."

Once Sam and Finn had disappeared with the mass of dishes that were almost scraped clean, Tess leant back with a contented sigh before taking a sip of her wine. They chatted about Tess's bakery and her growing custom cake business. Abby smiled as Tess excitedly described a fairy-themed wedding cake she was making.

"Goodnight, Aunty Abby," Finn interrupted. He padded over to Abby in his pyjamas, giving her a cuddle before moving around the table to say goodnight to his mum as well.

"Come on, Finn," Sam called from the kitchen door.

Abby laughed as Finn rolled his eyes and walked back, his shoulders slumped. "Have a good sleep," she said.

"I'm going to leave you ladies to chat while I do a bit of work," Sam called to them before ushering Finn back into the house.

"Sam's definitely a keeper," Abby said, turning her attention to Tess.

Tess's gaze remained fixed on the doorway for a moment before she turned to Abby. "That he is. I still can't believe I'm so lucky."

"You deserve every bit of happiness," Abby said, her heart swelling.

"What about you?" Tess asked.

Abby paused, wondering if she could get away with changing the subject again.

"You know you don't have to tell me anything," Tess said, her voice gentle. "But I'm here if you want to talk."

Abby played with the stem of her wineglass. She didn't know where to start, but she realised that she did need to talk to someone, and she didn't know anyone as supportive as Tess. "I think Quinn wants us to stay together beyond the summer," she said. She closed her eyes and tilted her face to the sky.

"You're admitting the pair of you are together now?" Tess asked, amusement clear in her tone.

Abby could tell that Tess was using teasing to help her find her way to whatever she needed to say. It was an approach she was more used to from her military friends. "Yes, okay, Quinn and I are together." She was surprised to find that the words felt right, as though something was settling around her that had been missing before.

"So, when you say you're together, what do you mean?" Tess asked.

"We spend every night together, we work together all day, and we're not hiding the fact that we're more than colleagues from the people we work with," Abby explained.

"Sounds serious," Tess said.

"It's not," Abby replied. The words were out before she could consider if they were true or not. "Quinn's spent so long avoiding his inherited job that he's not sticking around after the end of the summer, and I only have a job until Mrs Beaumont comes home from Canada." Abby paused, taking a sip of her wine, hoping it would ease the growing tightness in her chest. "There's no future I can see where we're together."

"Do you want there to be?" Tess asked.

Abby opened her mouth to say no, of course she didn't, but the words wouldn't form. "I don't know," she finally admitted.

"What's making you unsure?" Tess asked.

"I don't think I can settle anymore. I've spent my entire adult life moving from one place to another. The few months I spent at my parents' house were the longest I've been anywhere for years, and that was really tough."

"I know things were tricky with your parents," Tess said. "But it wouldn't be easy for anyone to move back in with their parents after a taste of independent life."

"To be honest, they were fine," Abby said. "You know my mum's obsession with me getting a job was a pain, but otherwise they were great. It was just being in the same place day after day. I just couldn't settle. It feels like I'll always be waiting for the next move."

"I can't begin to understand how hard the transition from military life is," Tess said. "Only you can know what is right for you, and whether or not that's Quinn, but do you mind if I share some thoughts with you?"

Abby nodded her agreement and Tess continued.

"Firstly, I wonder if that need to move on would be tempered if you find yourself in the right place, with the right person." Tess held her gaze, as if wanting to make sure Abby was okay with what she was saying. "Secondly, if that need to keep moving doesn't go away, perhaps the right person would be happy to move on with you." Points made, Tess lifted the bottle to top up both of their glasses.

Abby stared into the garden. "What if Quinn doesn't want to move on with me?"

"What if he does?" Tess countered. Her simple reply filled Abby with a wave of hope that she wasn't sure was healthy.

CHAPTER TWENTY-SIX

Walking back from Honeyford village, Quinn glanced at his watch and realised he really should have taken one of the estate vehicles. Despite his restless night, he'd woken up early, too fidgety to settle into anything, and had decided to walk down to the village so he could check the arrangements with the Angel Arms. Marsha had only been the landlady for a few years, which meant Quinn didn't have to deal with yet another person who'd known him in his youth, but the pub had partnered with Rose Hall for as long as Quinn could remember. The Angel Arms provided the bar for every Rose Hall event, and he was pleased to find that the slightly more specific requests made by Miles and India for their wedding hadn't caused Marsha too much trouble.

It was going to take Quinn the best part of an hour to make the journey back from the pub, and that was going to make him embarrassingly late for work. Part of him bristled at the fact that Abby somehow managed to make him feel guilty for not being at his desk on time, despite the fact he had been working, and that he was supposed to be head of the estate. Leaning forward to push over the stile, Quinn sucked in a deep breath, unimpressed with his own petty thoughts.

As he traipsed across the fields, barely aware of the building warmth of the day, he tried to work out just what he could say to Abby to prove that he was worth taking a chance on. Somehow, though, everything he came up with seemed trite.

Walking through the woodlands, Quinn followed the edge of the hedgerow, the peace of the summer morning broken by the loud whirring of a helicopter. Picking up his pace, he kept moving towards the house. There was only one reason he'd be able to hear that sound so close to the ground. Miles and India had arrived early.

Rounding the house, he strode past the stream of people who were setting up for the wedding, and headed towards the rear car park. The wind whipped ever stronger, giving some much-needed respite from the building heat as the chopper lowered to the ground. Touching down, the door slid open and Miles climbed out. As soon as his feet hit the ground, he turned and helped India out. Quinn felt his smile grow. If there was one thing that was destined to make this summer feel a success, it would be watching his friends get married, and playing a part in making it a wonderful event.

Head down, his hair whipped around as he hurried over to help with the bags that quickly followed, only to frown at the sight of Jacinda stepping out of the chopper. He should have guessed she'd come with India — after all, she was the maid of honour — but he hadn't registered that she'd be here so much earlier than the rest of the guests. At least in a crowd it was easier to manage her.

"Quinn!" Miles shouted, slapping Quinn's back as he joined them and lifted a couple of the large bags.

Jacinda simply left her luggage, all her efforts focused on attempting to keep her usually immaculate hair in place.

"Miles, we weren't expecting you until much later," Quinn said, once the helicopter had made its escape and they could hear each other.

"I know," Miles said. "But we were ready, and India couldn't wait to get here and make sure all the plans were in place."

"Everything is going to be perfect," Quinn said, pulling India in for a hug. "Abby is our events planner, and she is amazing."

"I think I spoke to her the other day," India said. "She certainly seemed to have everything in hand."

"She is so organised. Everything she's done this summer has gone fantastically well," Quinn said, smiling at the fact that India seemed a lot more relaxed than a bride might usually be. "I promise you, with her in charge your day will be wonderful."

Jacinda turned from her inspection of the property and studied Quinn. "We've missed you in the city, Tarquin," she said, leaning towards him in the way that Quinn knew meant she was waiting for a kiss on her cheek.

Taking a step towards her, he complied with the unspoken request, resisting the urge to roll his eyes at what she'd called him. He'd been named for a distant great-uncle, but he hated his full name so much that no one else ever used it. Unfortunately, Jacinda seemed to take great pleasure in doing so, regardless of how many times he had protested. Quinn turned back to India. "Why don't we get you set up in your bedrooms? Then I can take you to meet Abby."

"Perfect," India said. "We really can't thank you enough for letting us hold the wedding here."

"It's my mother you need to thank for that," Quinn said. "She's incredibly upset to be missing the big day after all the excitement of getting things ready."

"I think the arrival of her first grandchild is enough to forgive her absence," India said as she picked up one of the heavy-looking suitcases. "Now, lead the way."

Mr Heath dashed out and directed a couple of his team to help carry the cases upstairs. Leading the way to the first floor, Quinn smiled at India's expression when she took in the bedroom that she had been allocated for the next two nights.

"But…" she stuttered as she turned to face him. "This is the royal room."

Quinn laughed. Charles II was said to have spent a night at Rose Hall nearly four hundred years earlier, and it had been the royal room ever since.

"What's more regal than a bride on her wedding day?" he asked.

"But…" she started again. For a moment, Quinn was reminded that, despite their wealthy backgrounds, both Miles and India had been expected to make their own way in the world. They didn't have the same sense of entitlement that some of the rest of their social group had.

"No buts," Quinn said, pleased that Abby's suggestion had put such a look of delight on India's face. "The room doesn't get enough use as it is. You should enjoy it."

"Thank you," India said, wrapping her arms around his waist. "It's wonderful."

"You deserve it," he said, giving her a quick squeeze before stepping back and indicating the door opposite, which would be Jacinda's room. "Just so you know, it's only you ladies getting the special treatment tonight. I'm sticking Miles in Cordie's room for tonight. That way, you don't have to worry about bumping into him before the ceremony tomorrow."

"Thanks, Quinn," India said.

"That was Abby's idea as well," Quinn explained.

"Well, she's certainly living up to the glowing reference you've given her."

"She is special," Quinn said, knowing his anxiety about whether he'd be able to convince Abby to stay had crept into his tone.

"It's her job," Jacinda said with a sniff, her tone curt. "I'm not sure why we are praising someone for simply doing what they are paid to do."

Quinn frowned. He knew Jacinda was a little spoiled, but he hadn't heard her be so dismissive before.

"Shall we go and meet the lovely Abby?" India said, bouncing back up to Quinn and Jacinda after thoroughly inspecting her room.

Part of Quinn wanted to follow India's lead and skip towards Abby, as he hadn't seen her since she'd gone to Tess's yesterday afternoon. It was the longest they'd been apart since that first night in his room. However, he was also struggling with the fear that she'd leave him behind when her job here was done — a fear he'd have to face when he saw her.

They found Abby in the office, engrossed in work. She glanced up as the door opened, and took a more deliberate second look when she spotted Quinn. Her smile seemed to radiate across the room, and he wished they were alone so he could wrap her in his arms. Instead, he took a step to the side, gesturing so she'd realise he had brought company.

"Hello," Abby said, striding across the room, her arm outstretched. "You must be India."

"And you must be the amazing Abby," India said, shaking Abby's hand.

"I'm not sure about that," Abby said with a laugh, the sound sending warmth through Quinn's body. Without any conscious thought he moved, positioning himself at Abby's side.

"I am. You have been marvellous," India said, shooting a sideways glance at Miles. "And I would like to make it very clear that, contrary to what my fiancé has been telling everyone, we haven't arrived early because I was worried about the arrangements. I just couldn't wait to get here."

"You must be the groom," Abby smiled, reaching out to shake Miles's hand, before turning to Jacinda. "And you must be the lovely maid of honour."

Jacinda sniffed. Ignoring the hand Abby held out to her, she moved over to the table that Abby was using as her desk.

"I must say," Jacinda said, gesturing around her at the array of files and the long planner on the wall before sitting down. "This doesn't look particularly organised."

"I appreciate it might not look like it, but we do have a system," Abby said, and Quinn smiled at the hint of military abruptness that crept in at the criticism of her work.

"Abby is the most organised person I know," Quinn said, gesturing for everyone else to take a seat as well. "Shall I get some drinks and cakes?"

"Ooh, that would be great," India said, beaming.

"Tarquin, you shouldn't be doing that. Surely Abby should arrange it for us," Jacinda said, making it very clear she felt that was a job for the *staff*.

"I don't want to upset the boss," Quinn said, giving Abby a half smile, his cheeks warming as Abby raised her eyebrows in question and mouthed his full name. He had a suspicion that she was going to tease him relentlessly about it.

"But —" Jacinda started.

"Ah, so now we know what's been keeping you so busy all summer," Miles said before turning his attention to Abby, and Quinn silently thanked him for cutting off Jacinda. "How has your assistant been?"

"Oh, he's been alright," Abby said, laughing. "No, seriously, he's a natural. He would make a success of anything he put his effort into."

Quinn shifted, his gaze fixed on Abby as she spoke. As her eyes met his, he realised that she truly believed what she was saying. The level of faith she had in him filled his chest, forcing him to take a deep breath. Quinn realised that he would do whatever it took to keep Abby in his life. He wasn't sure he deserved such unwavering confidence, but he was determined to live up to it.

CHAPTER TWENTY-SEVEN

"Come with us," Quinn said, his words quiet, but Abby waved her arm.

"You go," she said, smiling.

Miles and India had made enough of an effort to get her to join them for a few drinks that Abby knew they meant it. Despite the small part of her that would have loved to accept, just to see that smirk wiped off Jacinda's face, she genuinely did have a lot to do before the next day and she wanted Quinn to be able to enjoy some time with his friends.

"You enjoy catching up with your friends, and I'll make sure we're set for tomorrow," she said, resting her hand on his arm. She wasn't used to this type of easy contact but found it hard not to touch Quinn when he was near.

"Are you sure?" he asked, ignoring the interested gaze of his friends.

"I'm sure, Tarquin," Abby said, waggling her eyebrows at him.

"You're never going to forget that that's my real name, are you?" Quinn asked with a sigh.

"Never."

"In that case, I'll see you later, *Abigail.*"

She laughed. "Well played, Quinn."

As they left the office, Abby watched Jacinda slip her arm through Quinn's. She glanced over her shoulder, as though wanting to make sure Abby had seen the movement. Allowing herself a small chuckle at the other woman's possessive behaviour, Abby pushed back on the small pulse of jealousy that tried to take over. Quinn had promised she didn't have to worry about other women, and Abby trusted him.

Forcing her attention back to the wedding plans, Abby was determined that nothing was going to spoil Miles and India's day. Weather permitting, the ceremony itself would be held in the formal gardens with the orangery as a backdrop, followed by the wedding breakfast in the restaurant, and then dancing in the ballroom. If the weather meant being outside wouldn't work for the ceremony, then they'd use the orangery itself. The place hadn't been used for years, but Jiro and his team had cut back the overgrowth, and the place had a kind of magical quality that made it feel like something out of a fairy tale. They'd have to bring all the chairs and floral arrangements in, but it would work, and at least any rain would dissipate the heat.

The rest of the evening passed in a flurry of activity, and if it hadn't been for Donna sending up a plate of sandwiches, Abby knew she'd have forgotten to eat. By the time she'd completed all of the tasks on her list for that evening, it was eleven o'clock.

Making her way up to the first floor, Abby paused at the top of the stairs as the sound of laughter drifted from the drawing room. Even though the room was part of the public tour, the family used it when they were formally entertaining. It was the first time it had been in use since Abby had arrived. It gave the whole floor a lovely feel, as though the house was coming to life. She knew she would be welcome to join the group, but the next day was going to be a busy one. Besides which, it would be good for Quinn to have some time to reconnect with his friends.

Waking the next morning, Abby smiled as she brushed Quinn's hair back from his forehead. He was sleeping so heavily that he didn't seem to register her movement as she forced herself out of his arms. It had been almost two o'clock in the morning before he'd joined her, and his whispered appreciation that she'd decided to sleep in his bed had been enough to rouse her from her disturbed sleep.

There had been a frantic, almost desperate feeling to the way he'd touched her, kissed her, loved her, and she'd tried to express how important he was to her with her own responses. Abby knew Quinn was working towards wanting to discuss their future, but she didn't have any answers. All she could do was hope to express how much she cared for him. Finally they'd both fallen asleep, and as was always the case when she was in Quinn's arms, her sleep had been deep and dreamless.

A quick glance at her phone let her know it was just before six o'clock. Plenty of time for a run before she had to get started on the day. Opening the door, she smiled as all three of Beatrice's dogs stirred, their heads swivelling up in unison.

Slipping down the corridor with her three companions, she was greeted by the sound of a deep, rattling snore, and she laughed at the realisation it was Miles. She was glad Quinn didn't snore. She wasn't sure she could spend the rest of her life sleeping next to someone who sounded like a chainsaw.

The thought pulled her up short, her strides along the hallway stopping. Where had that thought come from? Did she want to stay here? Did some part of her want her to be capable of having a future with Quinn? She forced herself to start moving again, determined to get to her room. Quinn had burrowed too far into her heart.

After quickly changing into a T-shirt, shorts and her trainers, Abby made her way down the back staircase, pulling her hair into a ponytail and chattering to the dogs as she went. The cool morning air was invigorating as she opened the door to the gardens. This was why she got up early. This feeling of stillness, the promise of the day to come always seemed so inspiring.

Arriving back at the house just over an hour later, pleased that the security team were already in place to prevent the newspapers from snapping unapproved photos, Abby worked through her cooldown stretches while the dogs lapped at bowls of water. Abby stood with her back to the building, letting her body recover as she soaked in the view. She might not be suited to settling anywhere, but there was a part of her soul that loved being here.

"And I thought I was up early." A soft voice interrupted Abby's meandering thoughts.

Turning, she smiled at the sight of India wrapped in a dressing gown, her hands curled around a steaming cup.

"I love this time of the day," Abby said.

"I can see why," India said, settling into one of the metal chairs on the small patio area by the door. "Although I must admit to being a bit too excited about the day ahead to appreciate it properly."

"Are you nervous?" Abby asked, genuinely curious about how it felt to make such a permanent commitment.

India reflected a moment. "A little. I love Miles completely, but it's a big step. No changing our minds after this."

"How do you know it's the right thing for you?" Abby asked, knowing she was creeping into territory that was inappropriate on India's wedding day, but unable to stop herself from asking.

India smiled. "I can't imagine my life without Miles in it."

The simple honesty of her statement made Abby pause. She had been so focused on her habit of moving on and how deeply rooted that instinct had become, that she hadn't considered what her life would be like after she left Rose Hall, after she left Quinn.

CHAPTER TWENTY-EIGHT

Watching Miles and India exchange their vows, Quinn felt his heart swell. Seeing his friends make the commitment to each other was something he knew he'd never forget. The love on their faces as they kissed for the first time as husband and wife made all the hard work of the last few days entirely worth it.

His gaze sought out Abby, standing there in a simple lemon dress with her hair pulled back into her standard bun. He didn't think he'd ever seen anyone look more beautiful. As usual, her outfit had sleeves long enough to cover her shoulders and upper arms fully, hiding the scars that she was embarrassed by. He hoped that one day she would see they simply added to her beauty, that they were a part of what made her the incredible woman she was. He hoped he'd be there to see that happen.

She didn't know these people, and yet her pleasure at how smoothly the ceremony was going was obvious. The smile she gave as she walked towards the newlyweds, ready to steer them to the side gardens for the first of the photos, seemed to make her glow. Despite arguing with Abby about it, she'd been determined that Quinn would only attend today as a guest and not as a member of the staff. Smiling, he remembered his attempts to persuade her that he should help out today. Lifting her against the shower tiles as they both abandoned any pretence at getting cleaned up had addled his brain enough that he hadn't been able to convince her, but it was definitely the most fun he'd had losing an argument.

Instead of following Abby and helping her get the photos arranged, Quinn let Jacinda slip her arm in his and lead the way to the patio, where champagne and canapés were waiting.

Ensuring Jacinda had a glass of champagne, Quinn made his excuses so he could check in with the rest of the Rose Hall team.

"I don't understand why you're bothering, Tarquin," Jacinda said, her hand resting on his arm. "They are your staff."

"Actually, they are my mother's staff," Quinn said, trying not to sigh at her insistence on using his full name. He'd tried to talk her out of it again last night, but she seemed determined to use it. "They are great people, and there is a lot to do today. I just want to make sure they are okay."

"Oh, that's very lovely of you. Just don't take too long," she said, her tone shifting, but not quite achieving the sweetness he suspected she was aiming for. "I've missed you this summer."

Forcing a smile, Quinn headed towards the kitchen. Had Jacinda always been so self-centred? He didn't remember that about her, but perhaps she had. He just wasn't sure he liked what that said about him, about who he'd been before this summer.

On his way to the restaurant entrance, Quinn was waylaid by Charlie. "Quinn," he said, his tone as awkward as he looked. "Could I have a word?"

Quinn nodded and smiled. He had gone to his last meeting with Charlie all excited about being able to help the business, but a little bit of time and distance had made him accept that he had been foolish to think his friend would see just how much he had changed. Quinn wasn't about to hold Charlie's reaction against him. He didn't blame the man for wanting to protect the business he'd worked so hard to build.

"I just wanted to apologise for how I reacted to your proposal," Charlie said, tugging at his collar.

"It's fine," Quinn said, realising he meant it.

"It's not. I was an ass, and I'm sorry. I'd like to hear your proposal."

"No, you were right. I'm not the right person to take on more for you," Quinn said, wanting to be clear there were no hard feelings. "I'll share my thoughts just in case you can make use of them, but I need to find my own place."

Charlie frowned, as though looking for some reassurance that Quinn meant what he said, before nodding. "I'd like that. You always have great ideas."

"For now, please excuse me," Quinn said. "You know what it's like, things to do."

As he walked through the restaurant, a quick glance around let him know that the tables had all been set to perfection. He suspected Donna had been out here with a ruler, checking that each place setting was precise. Looking around, Quinn wondered if he had already found his own place in the world.

"How is everything going?" Quinn asked as he pushed through the doorway to the kitchen. The place was buzzing with activity.

Donna glanced over from where she was overseeing the plating of the starters. "What are you doing in here? You're supposed to be enjoying the day with the rest of the guests. Abby has been very clear about that."

"That looks amazing," Quinn said, ignoring the question as he took in the delicately structured plates of roasted beetroot salad. "I just wanted to see if I could help with anything."

"Yes, just like that," Donna said, addressing one of her team before turning and giving him her full attention. She simply raised her eyebrows and waited.

"Fine," Quinn said. "I'm so used to working that it feels strange not to be part of the team today."

Donna's expression softened. "You are part of the team. You always have been."

"Just not a contributing member."

"Well, that has certainly changed," she said. "I thought you might have come back here to try and avoid the woman who is apparently draping herself over you at every opportunity."

"Have you been spying?" Quinn asked. "I thought you'd have been too busy back here for that."

"I have, but you know I have eyes everywhere. So, who is she, and why hasn't Abby smacked her one yet?"

It was the first time Donna had said anything about his relationship with Abby, and Quinn found himself fighting a smile at her obvious approval.

"Firstly, Jacinda is just a friend," Quinn said, with a roll of his eyes. "And secondly, if I was stupid enough to let anything happen, Abby would be more likely to smack me one, right before walking away from me."

"That's true. It doesn't mean Abby will enjoy that woman touching you so much, though."

"That's just the way Jacinda is with everyone," Quinn said with a dismissive shrug. "It doesn't mean anything. Anyway, is there anything I can help with?"

"No, honestly, we have everything under control. Thank you for taking the time to come and ask, though."

"That's what teammates do."

"So, does that mean you might stick around once your mother is back?" Donna asked.

The question made Quinn falter. He certainly wasn't ready to share that his thoughts kept heading in that direction. He had been so determined not to come back here, not to take a hereditary position he didn't deserve, that he wasn't sure how to admit that he didn't feel the same anymore. The realisation that he was asking for a commitment from Abby that he hadn't been ready to make himself settled uncomfortably. Shoving his hair out of his face as he headed back outside, Quinn accepted that he wasn't being fair. He wanted Abby to commit to him when he didn't know what he wanted, or what his life would involve. Despite his slowly shifting feelings about being at Rose Hall, he was certain of one thing: he wanted to be a part of Abby's future. Knowing that didn't help, though; he owed it to them both to work out who he wanted to be first.

Quinn was sure that the meal was delicious, but he barely tasted it. He needed to find Abby. He wasn't naïve enough to think that one conversation could resolve everything for either of them, but he needed to speak to her. He needed to know that there was some hope for the future. As long as he had that, he would trust that the rest would follow in time. The glimpses of Abby as she wove in and out of the restaurant area, speaking to their colleagues and chatting with guests, were a kind of torture, and yet he couldn't stop himself from looking for her.

"Tarquin," Jacinda said. The warmth of her palm on his thigh drew his eyes down to his leg.

Had she really always been this tactile? He'd said as much to Donna, but now he wasn't sure. Shifting his chair slightly so Jacinda had to pull her hand back, he forced his gaze up to meet hers.

"Are you worried the staff aren't up to the job?" she asked.

"No, they are all very good at what they do," he said, forcing a smile.

"Then here," she said, handing him a glass of wine that he was sure hadn't been as full a few moments before. "You need to stop watching them. You should relax and enjoy spending time with your friends."

Taking the glass from her, he took a small sip, relieved when Miles and India rose from their seats. The action was the cue that there would be an hour's pause in the festivities. Most of the guests had travelled in and would be spending the hour relaxing here or in the garden, but the bride and groom would be able to go to their room and enjoy their status as newlyweds before returning for the evening's events.

"I do need to go and help with the arrangements for later," Quinn said, ignoring the frown forming on Jacinda's face as he turned and walked out of the restaurant.

Swallowing hard, he tried to work out where Abby would be, and decided to start with the ballroom.

Before he could second guess himself, and his wisdom at attempting to discuss their future on an already busy day, he headed in that direction. Unfortunately, when he arrived, she was nowhere to be seen.

"Quinn!" a voice called.

Quinn turned to see Kelly, Barney's wife, heading towards him, her smile radiant. "What are you doing out here?" he asked with mock annoyance. "The guests are supposed to be in the restaurant area and outside."

"I couldn't resist taking a sneak peak," she said, as her hand cradled her prominent stomach. "I won't be able to do much dancing, so I thought I'd have a nosey before everyone else was in here."

"Definitely worth missing the dancing," Quinn said, realising that for the first time his words weren't just the socially appropriate platitudes. He was beginning to realise that he wanted a future like Kelly and Barney's.

As he was chatting to Kelly, a movement in the hallway caught his attention, and his gaze lifted to see Abby walking towards him. Her purposeful stride made his smile grow.

"Ah, I'd better let you get on," Kelly said, her gaze moving from Quinn's face to see where he was looking.

"Thanks, Kelly. I'll see you and Barney later," he said.

"Is everything okay, Quinn?" Abby asked.

He nodded, not able to trust his voice immediately. His efforts at reassuring her clearly hadn't worked, because she crossed the hallway quickly, slipping her hand into his and giving a quick squeeze.

The welcome sensation of her touching him spurred him into action. Keeping her hand firmly in his, Quinn led Abby down the corridor and slid into the first room they came upon. Glancing around, he realised it was the office that Lisa and a couple of the other admin staff would normally be occupying.

"What's wrong?" Abby asked, her brow furrowing and giving Quinn a glimmer of hope. Surely if she was as worried about him as her expression suggested, he must mean more to her than a casual fling.

"The other day, when you talked about not settling anywhere," Quinn began, blurting the words out while the renewed hope sustained him.

Abby's expression fell. Quinn's chest seemed to tighten as he took in the dismay that now covered her features. Before he could lose his nerve, he forced the rest of the words out. He needed to know, no matter how much this was going to hurt.

"Did you just mean places, or did you mean people as well? Did you mean you wouldn't settle down with someone? With me?"

Abby swallowed, her hand slipping from his. She opened her mouth but closed it again before anything could come out. Her gaze dropped to the floor. "I don't know," she said quietly.

Taking a step back, Quinn leant against the edge of one of the desks. He wasn't sure his legs could support him. He'd known he was taking a risk, but he was finally starting to feel like he was worth something, and part of that meant facing up to the reality of his relationship with Abby. Now he was here, though, he wasn't sure how he was going to survive this moment.

"Oops, sorry."

Quinn glanced up to see a smiling Lisa, her hands full with a tray of food as she pushed the door open.

"I was just planning to eat somewhere quiet," she said.

"It's fine," Quinn said, relieved that his voice was clear and steady. "We were just covering off some plans, but we're done now so you can eat in peace."

Without allowing himself to glance at Abby, he strode out of the room, determined to make sure Abby couldn't try to continue the discussion. She'd made her position clear, and he would respect that, but he knew he'd break completely if he had to listen to her try to explain.

CHAPTER TWENTY-NINE

The rest of the wedding passed in a blur. Despite continuing to try, Abby had been unable to get Quinn on his own. While everything about the wedding had gone perfectly to plan, the sight of Jacinda pinned to Quinn's side all evening had been enough to make her want to scream.

She needed to talk to him, to explain what she'd been trying and failing to say. She wanted to give this thing between them a chance, but she was terrified. That sense of needing to move on had become ingrained over the last decade, and she was scared of what it meant for any kind of long-term relationship.

By the time the majority of the guests had left, the large grandfather clock was striking one o'clock in the morning. Those remaining were gathered in a single group in the library, clearly all friends with the bride and groom. Was it really just last night that she'd been certain Quinn would have welcomed her if she'd joined his group? Now, she wasn't sure if anything she could say would be enough to allow them to get back to where they were. She wasn't even sure if she should try. Perhaps it would be kinder to them both for her to let him go.

"If you're sure you don't mind hanging on to sort taxis for the stragglers, I'm going to call it a night," Abby said, mustering a smile for Mr Heath.

"Of course I don't mind," he said. "Some of us didn't start work ridiculously early this morning."

"Thank you," she said, turning to go upstairs.

Abby couldn't stop herself from glancing into the library as she passed it. Although they weren't in there alone, it was clear that Jacinda and Quinn were having a private conversation.

The fact Jacinda had her hand on Quinn's leg was enough to make Abby want to storm in and demand that Quinn explain what he was playing at, but she didn't. The possessive feelings were foreign to Abby, and just added to the maelstrom of emotion that seemed to be churning through her.

Taking a deep breath, Abby forced herself to walk away from the library. The fact was, she wasn't sure if she and Quinn were together or not anymore. If they weren't, she had no right to feel the way she did.

Hauling herself up the stairs, Abby found herself standing at the door to Quinn's room, unable to decide whether or not she should go in and slip into his bed. The thought of Quinn coming in later and telling her she wasn't welcome made her lightheaded, but if she didn't go in, that would be making a statement she wasn't ready to make. It would be an explicit confirmation that whatever had been between them was over.

Abby pulled out her phone. A quick glance at the chat app let her know her brother was awake.

How are you lot doing? Abby tapped out the message and hit send.

Seconds later, Rob's reply appeared. *All good here. Can't wait until the monsters are back at school, though.*

Abby smiled at the thought of her nieces, and the fun they would have had driving Rob mad over the last few weeks. No matter what was going on in her life, her brother always made her feel as though she could cope, as though she could breathe.

Trouble sleeping again? he asked.

Abby decided to be honest. *Sort of. I met someone and I don't know what to do about it.* She let out a deep breath, not realising how much she'd needed to share that with Rob until she'd actually done it.

What? Who? What do you mean you don't know what to do?

Abby smiled. *Someone here at Rose Hall. I think they want something permanent, and I don't know if I can do it.*

It took a little longer for the reply to come through this time. *Don't know if you can, or don't know if you want to?*

Rob had got to the heart of the matter. Part of her was screaming that she had to try, that she'd regret it if she didn't. The other part of her, the part that lived with the guilt of lost colleagues and friends every day, didn't know if she could.

I'm not sure, she finally typed out.

Right, the girls and I will come and visit their Aunty Abby tomorrow.

For a moment, Abby considered telling Rob not to come — she was a grown woman who didn't need her big brother riding to her rescue. But the idea of seeing him and the twins was too much to resist.

That would be amazing, she replied.

In the meantime, don't close off any options, Rob messaged. *See you mid-morning.*

Holding the phone to her chest, Abby considered Rob's final remark. As always, confiding in him had helped. Turning the handle, she opened Quinn's door and pulled the curtains closed. Lifting a blanket off his bed, she crossed the room to the couch that ran along one wall. She might not feel comfortable getting into his bed, but she was going to make sure she was here when Quinn came up.

CHAPTER THIRTY

Groaning at the crick in her neck, Abby jerked upright. A quick glance across the room let her know that Quinn's bed hadn't been touched. Her stomach sank at the realisation he hadn't made it to bed, or — and her stomach sank further at this thought — he hadn't made it to his own bed. It was almost seven in the morning. Abby's sleep had been filled with her usual nightmares, though this time Quinn's face had been muddled in with everything.

Swallowing the nausea that rolled through her at the idea of where Quinn could have ended his night, Abby forced herself up. For the first time in as long as she could remember, she knew she wouldn't be able to run. Her usual determination had abandoned her. She'd have a shower and get dressed. It was going to take every ounce of her energy to get the newlyweds and their maid of honour through their departure breakfast without giving away any of her own emotions. At least she had Rob and the girls' visit to look forward to later.

Once dressed, Abby wondered what to do with her hair. She wanted to put it up in her normal bun, as a signal to everyone that she was fine, but she decided to leave it down, so she could use it as a shield. No matter what, she needed to make sure that no one saw anything except comfortable professionalism on her face this morning. She had a horrible feeling that witnessing Jacinda and Quinn together would make it much harder than anything she'd ever done.

Making her way through the house, Abby forced a smile as she passed the clean-up crew. Mr Heath had given some of his team the day before off, knowing that they would have their hands full today.

"It doesn't look quite the same this morning, does it?" Abby said to Mrs Barclay as the woman walked into the main hallway from the library.

"No," Mrs Barclay said. "The shine has definitely gone the morning after. Hopefully the bride and groom will sleep in, so it'll be in some sort of order by the time they come down."

"Fingers crossed," Abby said.

"Oh, and I've asked the staff to leave the library for now," Mrs Barclay added, as she walked towards the maze of corridors leading to her office. "Quinn is fast asleep in there."

Abby froze. After a moment, she started moving towards the library. Surely if Jacinda was in there with Quinn, Mrs Barclay would have mentioned that?

Leaning against the doorframe, Abby took in the sight of Quinn stretched out on the couch, his head at an angle and a blanket draped over his top half. He was still wearing his polished brogues. Abby's legs suddenly felt as though they couldn't take her weight. Quinn might not have made it to his own bed, but it looked as if he had spent the night alone.

"Thank you so much for everything," India shouted, holding both of Abby's hands in her own and smiling warmly as she tried to be heard over the immense noise of the helicopter. "I hope we can keep in touch."

"It has been our absolute pleasure," Abby said. "I'd love to keep in touch."

India bent over and ran to the helicopter, giving a final wave before Miles helped her climb inside. Waving off the happy couple and a grumpy Jacinda, Abby turned to Quinn. Miles had woken him and insisted they all had breakfast together.

Abby had managed to keep her churning emotions hidden throughout, something that was made a little easier by the fact Jacinda was clearly unhappy with Quinn.

As the helicopter disappeared into the distance, Abby finally had Quinn alone, and she searched for the words to explain herself.

"Quinn," she started, not sure what she was going to say.

"Don't," he said, holding up his hand, his face twisting with pain. "I just can't."

Before Abby could gather her thoughts, Quinn turned and started walking away. Knowing she couldn't force him to have a conversation he didn't want, she blurted out the first thing she could think of. "My brother is coming today," she called. "I'd like you to meet him."

Quinn stopped walking, and after a few moments he turned to face her, his expression blank. "You want me to meet your brother?"

"If you'd like to," she said, suddenly nervous.

Quinn held her gaze. Finally, he nodded, before turning and walking away again.

"Aunty Abby," Alice said, beaming a gappy smile at Abby. "My tooth fell out and the tooth fairy gave a pound."

"Wow, that's cool," Abby said, breaking off her conversation with Rob to give her niece attention.

"It is, and sometimes I have cold hands, and sometimes I always have hot hands," Alice said.

"And what are they like at the moment?"

"Hot," Alice said, placing a slightly sticky and overly warm hand on each side of Abby's face.

"They are definitely warm," Abby said with a laugh, grabbing her niece around the waist so she could pull her into her lap and tickle her.

Alice's giggles brought Betty running over, and soon Abby was fighting off two small girls intent on tickling her in return.

Once the twins had tired of this, they ran off in search of the fairies their dad had assured them lived in the array of stripped logs that were set out in this part of the grounds as a kind of obstacle course.

"That's mean," Abby said. "They'll be so disappointed when they can't find any fairies."

"It's sensible parenting," Rob said. "They'll get distracted by something and forget all about the fairies, and in the meantime, I get a bit of peace and quiet."

"You love having the girls around," Abby said with a smile.

"Fine," Rob said, with mock reluctance. "I do love getting to spend so much time with them, but I will be glad when the summer holidays are over and we're all back to school."

"Still enjoying it, then?" Abby asked.

Even when they'd been children, Rob had wanted to be a teacher and Abby had been incredibly proud of him when he'd started his job.

"Yes, I love it," he said. "I'm glad I do primary school, though. I'm not sure I'll enjoy these two as much when they are teenagers and have an answer for everything." He turned to face Abby and raised his eyebrows. "So, who's the guy then?"

Abby glanced around, making sure they were alone before turning back to Rob. "It's Quinn Beaumont," she said.

"Quinn Beaumont?" Rob asked, frowning. "As in, the heir to this place, the guy who's always in the gossip magazines?"

"He's not like they make him out to be," Abby said, nervous to talk about her feelings but determined that Rob wouldn't judge Quinn by what he'd read. "Besides which, since when do you read gossip magazines?"

"You know Fiona loves them, and I can't resist a little flick through now and then," Rob said with an unembarrassed shrug. "Have you seen any of the press coverage about him?"

"Yes," Abby said, resisting the urge to roll her eyes. "I promise you he's not the man you've read about."

"Alright," Rob said. "I'm going to worry about you getting involved with someone with his reputation, though."

"Rob," Abby said, her tone making her annoyance clear.

"Look, I understand you want to defend him, but I was worried about you working with him. I'm only going to be more worried now. However, I trust your judgement." Circling his hand in front of his chest, Rob urged Abby to continue.

"I don't know where to begin," she said.

"Are you sleeping with him?"

"Are you sure you want to know?" Abby asked with a mischievous smile.

"God no," Rob grimaced. "But if you want my advice, which obviously you always do, then I need to know how far into this relationship you are."

"I don't have nightmares when he's there," Abby said softly.

Rob leant back in his chair, his eyes widening. "You love him."

"I —" Abby began, about to deny it, but she realised that a denial might not be entirely honest. Sinking back into her own chair, she rubbed her face. "I don't know."

"So, what's the problem?"

"I don't know if I can do it."

"Do what?" Rob frowned.

"Commit to someone, to somewhere," Abby said.

"You're worried you'll get bored?" Rob asked, as always cutting to the heart of her worries.

Abby simply nodded.

"How does Quinn feel?" Rob asked.

Abby frowned. "I don't know. I think I messed up."

"Messed up how?"

"I said something about not knowing if I will stick around because I don't usually. When he asked me if I would consider sticking with him, I said I didn't know." Abby's gaze fell to the ground.

"Is that because you don't want to stick with him, or because you've spent so long moving around that you don't know if you can stick at anything?"

Abby looked up at Rob. She should have known her brother would understand. "The second one," she said quietly.

"Only you can decide if Quinn is worth taking a chance on," Rob said. "But it seems like you want to try, because if you didn't, you wouldn't be feeling so confused."

Abby nodded again. "I'm scared," she said, not sure where she'd found the strength to make that admission, but knowing that it was the truth.

CHAPTER THIRTY-ONE

The second his mobile rang, Quinn snatched it up. The estate was closed for the day to give them all time to get organised again after the wedding, and he'd been trying not to walk around the house, seeking out Abby and her brother. The idea of her wanting him to meet her family was tantalising, as though perhaps they might have a chance. It was close to one o'clock, and Abby was finally calling him.

"Hi, Quinn," Abby said once he answered the phone, her tone uncertain.

"Hi, Abby," he said, keeping his own determinedly light. "How is your visit with your family going?"

"Great, thank you. Would you like to join us for lunch? We're in the picnic gardens."

"I'd love to," Quinn said, the words coming out in a rush of relief. "Do you have the picnic with you, or shall I bring it out?"

"Just come out," Abby said. "The girls are busy playing, so we'll get the food when we're all ready."

Quinn strode out of the office, his legs feeling wobbly as his nerves built. Halfway down the corridor, he took a moment to check his reflection in one of the large gilt mirrors. He couldn't do much about the bags under his eyes, or the grey tinge to his complexion from spending most of last night drowning his sorrows, but at least his hair was behaving reasonably well. His white shirt and khaki chinos were casual enough to suit a picnic. Were they the right choice to impress Abby's brother, though? Given Abby's strength of character, it didn't really make sense, but Quinn couldn't shake the feeling that getting her brother's approval could change his future.

Once outside, Quinn smiled at the two little girls who were romping around the play area. Even if the place had been full of tourists, their red hair would have given away that they were Abby's nieces.

"Hello," he said, squaring his shoulders and taking a deep breath as he approached Abby and her brother.

"Hi, I'm Rob." Rob stood and shook Quinn's hand.

Rob's frame was slight and he was shorter than Quinn, but the steely look in his eye was still unnerving. It was clear that Rob took his big brother duties seriously.

"Lovely to meet you," Quinn said. "Abby speaks very highly of you."

"Oh, does she?" Rob asked with a smile, turning to Abby with his brows raised.

"Don't get big-headed," she replied. "I simply told Quinn that you're not bad as big brothers go."

"Of course you did," Rob said, giving her an exaggerated wink. Abby reached over and shoved him.

Once Rob sat back down, Quinn did the same and gestured to the girls.

"They look like they are having a lovely time," he said.

"They are," Rob sighed. "And they're burning off energy, which will make it easier to convince them to go to bed tonight."

"It's lovely that you've been able to come and visit Abby," Quinn said, slipping his sunglasses on. "We think a great deal of her here." He smiled inwardly at the way Abby's cheeks pinked; he knew she wasn't great with compliments.

"I'm not surprised," Rob said, rolling his eyes. "It's an annoying quality in a little sister, but apparently she's great at everything she does."

"Well, one of us has to be," Abby replied cheekily, glancing over the top of her sunglasses.

Quinn found himself quickly relaxing; the easy banter between the siblings settled his nerves enough for him to enjoy himself, despite how important Rob's opinion of him remained.

"Aunty Abby, we're starving!" The little girls ran up, shouting in unison.

Abby's face lit up as she watched them approach, and Quinn realised that he could spend the rest of his life seeing Abby that happy. The girls gave him one curious glance, before returning their focus to far more important things. Each of them taking one of Abby's hands in theirs, they pulled her to her feet.

"Come on, Aunty Abby. Let's go and get the picnic," they said, pulling at her.

"Alice and Betty," Rob said, his voice stern. "Where are your manners?"

The pair studied him with identically curious looks.

"Don't you think you should say hello to Mr Beaumont?" Rob asked, gesturing to Quinn.

"Sorry, Daddy," they both said, before walking over to Quinn.

"Hello, Mr Beaumont. I'm Alice. It's nice to meet you," the twin in the pink shorts and green camouflage T-shirt said.

"And I'm Betty," the twin in a blue polka dot dress with a pair of camouflage socks said.

Both of them beamed at Quinn, and he felt his heart melt a little. They were absolutely adorable, and clearly as independent and confident as their aunt.

"Hello, it's lovely to meet you both too, and you can call me Quinn. Thank you for coming to visit today," he said, beaming back at them, before leaning a little closer and whispering, as though sharing some big secret, "I think your aunty really missed you."

They both nodded seriously, before turning and running back to Abby.

"Can we go and get the food now?" Alice asked. "We're soooo hungry."

"Come on, then," Abby said, smiling broadly despite the shadows under her eyes, the ones Quinn suspected he'd put there. "You two can help me carry it."

Suddenly, Betty ran back over to Quinn, her voice quiet as she asked what was clearly a very important question. "Is there cake in the picnic?"

Quinn laughed. "I don't know, but if there isn't, you will find lots of cakes in the storeroom with the big blue door," he said, giving them a wink. "Make sure you take as many as you would like."

Rob gave him a mock frown and muttered something about their mum murdering him if they ate too much sugar, but he didn't protest. Abby and the little girls headed to the kitchen.

"So," Rob said, turning and focusing on Quinn in a way that made him want to squirm. He had a feeling this was the point at which Abby's dad would be threatening him with a shotgun, and her brother was simply here holding his place. "What are your intentions towards my sister?"

Quinn felt a slightly hysterical urge to laugh. There would be no subtlety here. "I love her, and I want a future with her," he said simply, lifting his sunglasses off so that Rob could see the sincerity of his words.

"What about the press stories about you?" Rob asked.

Quinn's heart sank a little. "I'd like to say that none of that is true," he said, working up to admitting what he'd much rather keep to himself. "But to be honest, some of it is. I have been pretty directionless for a long time. Because of that, I've spent a lot of time partying, and yes, a lot of what you will have read is true. Well, except for the rehab thing. I've never done drugs."

Quinn glanced back at Rob, who didn't reply. He just nodded, as if inviting Quinn to continue.

"The last few months have changed all of that," Quinn said, pushing his hair back and holding Rob's gaze. "Abby has changed that."

"How?" Rob asked.

"Abby has helped me see what I'm capable of. She's helped me to feel comfortable with who I am," Quinn said, the words coming out with urgency as he fought to make Rob see just how serious he was. "She is strong and capable and doesn't take any nonsense from anyone. I love her."

"And how do you think she feels about you?"

"I don't know. I want to believe she feels the same way, but I just don't know."

"And if she doesn't?"

Quinn did look away at that, not able to deal with the raw pain that flooded his body. He had to take a few deep breaths before he could reply. "Then I'll respect that that's her decision," he finally said.

"Okay," Rob said, finally nodding. "Okay."

It wasn't exactly a ringing endorsement, but Quinn was taking it as a good sign. Focusing on controlling his breathing, he tried to push away the awful feelings that had come all too easily at the thought of Abby not wanting to be with him. They sat in silence for a few minutes before Rob spoke again.

"You know about Abby's past?" he asked.

Quinn turned back to Rob and nodded.

"Then you know that for over a decade, she hasn't been in the same place for more than a few months." Rob paused. "You know that she has lost people she was responsible for in the army."

Quinn nodded again.

"She's scared," Rob said.

Quinn frowned; he'd never met anyone less likely to be scared than Abby.

"I know what you're thinking," Rob said, giving him a wry smile. "But I promise you, she's scared."

"Of what?" Quinn asked.

"That she's not capable of staying somewhere, or with someone, for long. She's scared that if she tries, she'll hurt too much when it ends."

"But —" Quinn started, but Rob gave a sharp shake of his head, indicating that Abby was on her way back to them.

"If you love her," Rob said, the words quiet, his lips barely moving. "Don't let her fear stand between you."

"What have you two been talking about?" Abby asked, her tone suspicious as she placed a huge picnic hamper on the table between them.

"Oh, you know, just telling Quinn here about your childhood escapades," Rob said. "I was just going to tell him about when you threw up all over the vicar."

"No, you definitely aren't going to share that story," Abby said as she opened the hamper.

Quinn stood and started pulling out an array of treats. It looked as though Abby had used a lot of the extras from yesterday's wedding breakfast and evening nibbles. The girls came up to his side, carrying a second hamper.

"We found some cakes," Betty said, her face shining with glee.

"Excellent," Quinn said.

"Abby spent the whole of Sunday school secretly stuffing herself with toffees and chocolates from a box she'd found in the cupboard that the Brownies used," Rob was saying, the words coming out in bursts as Abby tried to cover his mouth with her hand. "She made herself so sick that when we were back with our parents and the vicar was saying goodbye to everyone outside, Abby threw up all over him."

"Cool," Betty said, her eyes widening before turning to the hamper of cakes.

"Betty," Rob called, pulling his daughter's attention back to him, "if you eat so much cake that you throw up, I'll start listening to your mother and make you wear the outfits she chooses."

Betty gave her father the sort of glare that, with a few more years behind it, would terrify any recipient, but Rob's eyes glittered with amusement.

By the time Rob, Alice and Betty were saying their goodbyes, Quinn still hadn't managed to get Abby's brother alone again.

"Thank you for having us," the girls chorused after being reminded to use their manners again.

"You're welcome anytime," Quinn said with a smile.

Rob pulled Abby in for a long hug, clearly whispering something to her, before shaking Quinn's hand. "Remember what I said," he said, the words so quiet that Quinn knew Rob hadn't wanted Abby to pick them up as well.

He climbed into his car, and the girls' little hands came out of the back windows, waving frantically until they disappeared around the bend in the driveway.

"Thank you for making them so welcome," Abby said, turning to him, her expression slightly guarded.

"They are great," Quinn said.

Rob hadn't said a lot, but it was clear that he thought Abby might have feelings for Quinn. Knowing this, Quinn couldn't give up on them, not yet. He did, however, need to change his approach, because what Rob had said about her being scared had sunk in deeply. If he was going to have any chance of a future with Abby, he needed to ease her towards that, rather than confronting her for an on-the-spot decision.

"I've missed you," he said.

She swallowed. "I've missed you too," she finally admitted.

The relief that washed through him meant that he moved without any conscious instruction from his brain. His arm slipped around her waist, and he placed his lips on hers, determined to show her just how special she was to him.

CHAPTER THIRTY-TWO

"What are we going to do?" Mrs Barclay asked.

Abby wondered if she realised that she was turning to Quinn for answers. It was a major turnaround from the way she had treated Quinn at the start of the summer. Given how much he'd achieved in the space of a few months, Abby wanted to be around to see what he'd do in the years to come. She wanted to trust that she was capable of it, because the pain she'd felt last week when she'd believed their relationship was over had been intense. She knew she wouldn't survive if they tried for longer and it didn't work.

"Well, we need to find a different charity," Quinn said.

Rose Hall had held a very successful annual fundraising dinner and auction for an overseas aid charity for the last few years. This year, it was due to happen on the coming Friday evening. This morning, the charity had been exposed on the national news for exploiting those they were supposed to help, and for fraudulently spending some of their funds on luxury lifestyles for their leaders.

"But who?" asked Mrs Barclay. "People bought their tickets on the basis it was raising money for overseas aid. They won't want to come now."

The impromptu managers' meeting had happened without anyone needing to schedule it. As they had each arrived on site for the day, the managers had made their way directly to Quinn and Abby's office and were now blurting out a list of things they should do as damage control.

"We need to agree what the team should say if any press call," Mrs Barclay said. "And we need to prep them now."

"I'll have to see if I can cancel the food orders," Donna said, her fingers tapping on the desk in front of her.

"We'll need to contact all the people who bought tickets," Mrs Barclay added.

Mr Heath and Jiro just sat watching the growing panic of those around them, their expressions stricken.

"At least I can freeze the excess meat," Barry said.

"We are not cancelling this event," Quinn said, his tone so firm that everyone stopped muttering.

In the silence that followed, everyone studied Quinn expectantly.

"Abby, do you know any reputable veterans' charities?" he asked.

"Um, yes," she said, trying to process the direction he was taking them in.

"Why a veterans' charity?" Mrs Barclay asked.

"We will be contacting everyone who's bought a ticket and offering them a refund," Quinn said, ignoring the question, his gaze remaining on Abby. "And we will call every person or company who has donated to the auction and offer them the chance to withdraw their contribution."

"But we probably won't even get enough people who decide they still want to attend to cover our costs, never mind what that'll leave for the auction, and the work it'll take to redo all the auction materials."

Quinn's expression hardened as he turned to Mrs Barclay. "We will make it very clear that we are as distressed as they are about the news, but that we are delighted to be able to ensure that the event can go ahead for a thoroughly good cause." He turned, fixing his gaze on each of the assembled group in turn. "Abby and I are going to need help to call everyone quickly enough, though, so we will need each of you to spare someone from your own departments today. They will be advising that we have selected a veterans' charity because Rose Hall now has a very personal connection to someone who has served."

Abby had to look away as, blinking hard, she tried to stem the moisture that was threatening to spill down her cheeks. She wasn't surprised that within moments Quinn had solved the problem of the forthcoming event — it was the fact that his thoughts had instantly turned to something so personal, so important, to her.

"Abby, could you reach out to whichever charity you think is best? We need to make sure they are happy to partner with us before we speak to anyone else," Quinn said, drawing her attention back.

Abby nodded and dialled her old captain, who she knew would have the right contacts.

Within twenty minutes, Rose Hall had a new charity to support. An hour after that, a quarter of the attendees and contributors had been contacted, all of whom were happy to remain a part of the event.

"I can't believe no one has taken the refund option," Abby said, smiling at the assembled team, all of whom were busily making calls and notes.

"I can," said Quinn. "It's a great cause, and, if we wanted to be a bit cynical about it, most people just want a decent night out."

"I suppose you've been to a few of these sorts of things," Abby said, giving him a wry smile.

"I have," he said. "And I hate to admit it, but I couldn't have told you what the funds were being raised for at most of them. Not everyone is as shallow as I was, but quite a few people just want to attend to look important when bidding on the auction, and so they can say they were there."

"That really is cynical," Abby said, rolling her eyes at him.

"I know, and I really hope that most people are better than I am."

"You're not that person anymore."

"I hope not," Quinn said.

"Okay, that'll do for today." Quinn raised his voice enough to catch everyone's attention.

The team all turned to him, and Abby smiled at the ease with which he was leading them. For the first time since they'd started working together, he was taking the leadership role, and it suited him.

"I wanted to say a huge thank you for all of your hard work today," he said, beaming at them all. "You have helped us make sure that something which could have been a complete disaster for Rose Hall has become something positive. Now, go home and enjoy your evenings."

"Bye, Quinn. Bye, Abby," a chorus of voices called as they gathered up their personal belongings and headed out for the evening.

"That went well," Abby said, walking across the room to study the sheets on the wall. There were a few gaps on each, where the relevant person hadn't been contactable today, but the remainder was certainly small enough for her and Quinn to manage together. "We could try and contact a few of these ourselves later this evening." She turned to face Quinn, who was walking towards her with that half smile on his face. "You were brilliant." Her body grew warm as the contentment in his expression shifted into something more intimate.

"So were you," he said, stopping so close to her that she could feel his breath on her face.

"We make a great team," Abby said, the words spilling out before she could stop them. She was being extremely careful not to say anything that could reopen the conversation about the future.

"We do," Quinn said, slipping one hand around her waist, and the other into her hair. Steering gently, he manoeuvred them until Abby's back was against the wall, the slight rustle of the papers stuck there barely registering.

Abby kissed him, hoping that her action expressed just how much she cared about him, even though she shied away from putting her feelings into words.

Just as the hand on her waist moved, pulling her blouse out of her waistband, the door swung open and there was an awkward cough.

"Apologies," Mrs Barclay said. "I just wanted to run through tomorrow's tasks to make sure we would still be ready for Friday. I can come back later."

Abby felt heat rise up her neck. She loved that Quinn was happy for people to know they were more than just colleagues, but being caught like this definitely felt like crossing a line.

Quinn sighed and rested his forehead on hers. "To be continued later," he whispered.

Even as Abby grew warm at his words, her stomach twisted at the reminder that they were going to run out of time far sooner than she was ready for.

CHAPTER THIRTY-THREE

A few days later, Abby and Quinn were sitting with Tess at the Angel Arms pub in Honeyford, and Abby was opening an envelope she'd received that morning.

"What is it?" Tess asked, sipping her iced tea.

"It's authorisation to visit the Langport rifle range. It's not too far from here," Abby smiled.

"Is that from your old captain?" Quinn asked.

"Yes. It's a thank you for getting his charity associated with Rose Hall. Although I would think you deserve something for that more than I do."

"You deserve it," he said. "I'm just glad that you could put us in touch with a charity, and that the dinner and auction went so well."

"Didn't I read something in the local paper about you breaking last year's record?" Tess asked.

"We did," Quinn beamed.

"Do you think you'll stick around once your mum is back?" Tess asked, unwittingly taking the conversation in a direction Quinn had been trying to avoid.

"I don't know," Quinn said, realising that the only thing he could do was be honest. However, he couldn't risk scaring Abby off. "I've really enjoyed this summer, but I've spent so long fighting against just being the heir, I'm not sure if I'm ready to admit defeat and take on the job."

He almost groaned when Abby stiffened slightly, but thankfully Tess was astute enough not to push any further, instead changing the subject to the rapidly approaching end of summer ball.

"What are you wearing, Abby?" Tess asked.

"Oh, I hadn't thought about it," Abby said. "Probably just a suit."

"You need a ballgown," Tess said, smiling.

"I'll be working," Abby said with a roll of her eyes. "No one will care what I wear."

"I wouldn't say no one," Tess said with a laugh, tilting her head towards Quinn.

"He'll be working as well," Abby said. "Besides which, I'll be busy. The last time I wore a fancy dress, I could barely move in it, and don't even get me started on the lack of pockets. So definitely no ballgown for me."

Quinn smiled, his mind snapping straight to the night she was talking about. She might have found moving around in that dress difficult, but he'd had a thoroughly delightful time helping her out of it. Watching her until her gaze met his, he was pleased to see that familiar pink deepen on her cheeks. The fact she was remembering the same thing he was thrilled him. They might not have the future sorted, but the here and now was working perfectly.

Tess insisted on dropping them back to the estate on her way to deliver some cakes to the retirement community. As they were stepping out of her car, Quinn's phone rang.

"Hello, Mother," he said.

"Hello, Quinn," Beatrice said, her beaming face filling the screen. "I heard how well the auction went, and after all that drama, I am so proud of you."

"It wasn't just me," Quinn said, looking up to meet Abby's gaze as she finished waving goodbye to Tess. "Abby was amazing, and everyone chipped in to help. It was a real team effort."

"Is Abby there?" Beatrice asked, something in her tone shifting. "I'd love to thank her personally as well."

"Yes, she's here," Quinn said, gesturing for Abby to join him.

"Hello, Mrs Beaumont," Abby said, her tone warm.

"Now, dear, I thought we'd cured you of that Mrs Beaumont nonsense," Beatrice said.

"Sorry, Beatrice," Abby corrected herself. "How is your visit going? How are your daughter and granddaughter doing?"

Quinn smiled as his mother's face lit up. Abby certainly knew how to get her on side. Listening to his mother chatter about her new grandchild, he let himself enjoy the sensation of Abby's arm resting against his as she ensured she was close enough for both of their faces to appear on the small screen.

"Is this Abby?" Cordelia's face appeared next to Beatrice's, and Quinn resisted the urge to groan. He knew he'd talked about Abby too much in the last few calls he'd had with his sister and mother. There was no way that they didn't know how he felt about the woman at his side.

Deciding not to worry about it for now, he let himself enjoy the easy way the three of them were chatting, realising that if he managed to convince Abby, she would fit in perfectly with his family. The thought made him pause. All he could hear was his blood rushing in his ears as he realised he didn't just want Abby to give them a chance beyond this summer. He wanted forever with her.

"Quinn," Abby said, in the tone of someone who had been attempting, and failing, to get his attention for some time.

"Sorry," he said, shaking his head. "Managed to distract myself."

"That's okay," Abby said. "I'm going to let you have some private catch-up time with your family. We can cobble something together for dinner when you're done."

"You don't need to go," Quinn said, wanting to keep Abby by his side.

"I do," Abby said, raising her eyebrows at him. "I'm sure you all have things to talk about that you don't want me loitering around for."

He watched her as she walked towards the side entrance of the house, before turning his attention back to his phone.

"Are you going to tell us?" Cordelia asked.

Quinn frowned. Moving towards one of the picnic tables, he sat down. "Tell you what?" he asked.

"What's going on with you and Abby," Cordelia said.

"Who told you?" Quinn asked. "Honestly, you'd think the staff here would be too busy to have time to gossip."

As he finished speaking, he took in the look on his sister's face. It was a look he was all too familiar with, and one that let him know he'd fallen for one of her schemes.

"No one told you," he said flatly.

"Well, you just did," Cordelia laughed.

"Is it serious?" his mother asked.

Quinn considered making light of the situation, but he realised that he wanted to talk about it. He was in love with Abby, and he didn't want to hide that. "I'd like it to be serious," he said.

"So, why isn't it?" Beatrice asked in that no-nonsense tone that was so familiar. "She obviously likes you."

"She does?" Quinn asked, feeling stupid the moment the question was out. The fact that Abby spent almost every night in his bed was a pretty big clue that she liked him.

"The way you look at each other is a little bit disgusting," Cordelia said. "I'm pretty sure no sister should be expected to watch that."

"Cordelia," their mother reprimanded, and Quinn took the opportunity to stick his tongue out at his sister.

"Quinn," Beatrice said. "You clearly care for each other, but you need to talk to her if you want things to work out. Don't go doing all this modern, being too embarrassed to ask for what you want nonsense."

What could only be described as the sound of a hundred screeching cats started up.

"Mia is awake," Beatrice said. She turned to Cordelia. "I'll go and see to her. You catch up with your brother and tell him about our surprise."

"Does Mia do that a lot?" Quinn asked.

Cordelia rubbed under her eyes. "More than I'd like. I can't tell you how grateful I am to you for covering this summer so Mother could come here. I think I would have gone mad by now if I'd had to do this without her."

"Well, I was bullied until I didn't have any choice," Quinn smiled. "Anyway, what surprise?"

"Never mind that, now she's out of the way," Cordelia said, glancing behind her. "Tell me all about you and Abby."

CHAPTER THIRTY-FOUR

Watching as Quinn shuffled a pile of files for what was probably the fifteenth time, Abby decided to take pity on him.

"Quinn, why don't you go and see if Mr Heath has all the bedrooms sorted?"

"Oh, yes," Quinn said. "Good idea. I need to check if they've been able to set up the cot as well."

Placing an absentminded kiss on Abby's head, Quinn strolled out of the room.

"You know that everything is sorted upstairs, don't you?" Lisa asked, once Quinn was safely out of earshot.

"I do," Abby nodded. "But it'll take him a good thirty minutes to get up there, check every detail in every room, and get back down here."

"I like your style," Lisa said. "I definitely can't concentrate with him coming over and double-checking things all the time."

"He's just excited that his family are arriving home today," Abby said, defending him despite the way his nerves were winding her own uncomfortably tight. Since Quinn had told her that his mother would be back earlier than expected, and that she was bringing his sister and niece with her, Abby's insides had twisted. The summer was almost over. Her time with Quinn was almost over.

She wondered what the presence of the Beaumont family might do to their relationship. For someone who usually prided herself on being forthright, Abby hadn't found the courage to ask Quinn what was going to happen after today. She was scared she'd hear an answer she didn't like, but she also didn't know what answer she did want. She didn't even know where she'd be spending her remaining nights at Rose Hall.

"I'm surprised that Mrs Beaumont is coming back so soon, though," Abby said to Lisa, wondering if Beatrice wasn't as pleased with how the summer had gone for the estate as she professed to be. After all, there was only the forthcoming bank holiday weekend, followed by the end of summer ball to go.

"I don't think Mrs Beaumont has missed the end of summer ball in years," Lisa said.

Lisa's response reassured Abby slightly. Their phones beeped almost simultaneously — the estate WhatsApp group Abby had set up was proving useful. At the news that Mrs Beaumont's taxi was winding its way up the drive, Lisa's face lit up.

"We'd better go and greet them," Abby said, forcing a smile.

The pair of them stood and made their way towards the front of Rose Hall. The entire staff stood gathered to welcome Mrs Beaumont home, talking animatedly to one another. Realising she wasn't up to happy chit-chat while they each waited for a chance to greet Mrs Beaumont, Abby touched Lisa's arm.

"I'm just going to pop to the toilet before I come out," she said.

By the time Abby had come back out, Mrs Beaumont, Cordelia and baby Mia were out of the car and surrounded by a sea of heads. Standing slightly back from the group, Abby waited, not sure what she would say to her.

After a few minutes, baby Mia started to grizzle and Mrs Beaumont, clearly a doting grandparent, decided this was the time for them to make their way indoors.

"Oh, Abby dear," Mrs Beaumont said, as the assembled people moved so she could get to the house. "How marvellous to see you. You and I shall have a proper catch-up later, when I've had a chance to freshen up."

"That would be lovely," Abby said, trying to ignore the swooping sensation in her stomach.

"Now, Quinn," Mrs Beaumont said, turning back towards the car. "Would you be a dear and get someone to bring the smaller cases up now? They have all of Mia's things in them."

Without waiting for confirmation, Mrs Beaumont disappeared into the house.

It was almost four o'clock when Abby was summoned to meet with Mrs Beaumont in her private lounge. Abby hadn't seen Quinn since his mother had returned, and she needed to ask him whether she knew they had been more than colleagues these last few weeks. Now, she was having to face Mrs Beaumont unprepared.

The door to the private lounge was open, and Mrs Beaumont smiled broadly at the sight of Abby in the doorway, gesturing for her to come in.

"Please take a seat," she said. "Sorry, I'll just be a minute, there is always so much for me to sign when I've been away."

Abby sat at one end of the gilt-edged couch. It reminded her of the sort of thing you'd see in a French period drama, but the embroidered covers were faded, and any padding was long since gone. It was uniquely uncomfortable.

"Ah," said Mrs Beaumont, in a tone that made it clear Abby hadn't managed to hide her grimace entirely. "Sorry, everything in here is stuff that's so far past its best we can't use it on display in the areas we open to the public. It's all damned uncomfortable, but I can't bring myself to throw it out."

"It's fine," Abby said, conjuring a smile from somewhere.

"Now, then," Mrs Beaumont said. "How have you found things?"

"It's been really great," Abby said, grateful they were at least starting on a safe topic. "Your team here are amazing, and you had already done most of the work for the events, so everything went really smoothly. I would like to thank you for giving me this opportunity, Mrs Beaumont. It was just what I needed."

"Beatrice," Mrs Beaumont said, her tone firm.

"Beatrice," Abby said, her smile coming more naturally.

"And how has Quinn been?"

"He's amazing," Abby said, wondering if she should, or even could, temper her enthusiasm but deciding against it. "He's capable, the team here love him, and he's done an amazing job. I know he's the heir, but even without that, he's a real asset to this estate."

Abby realised she'd used the word amazing twice in one sentence, and that she was edging very close to giving away just how unprofessional some of her feelings for Quinn were, but she also realised she didn't care. She'd let Quinn's mother take what she wanted from her comments, as long as she realised that Abby was right. Quinn was so much more than the labels people gave him, and so much more than even he believed he was.

"Him being here hasn't made things more difficult for you?" Mrs Beaumont asked.

The question was casually spoken. For a brief moment, Abby wanted to say yes, Quinn being here had made things difficult for her. Quinn made her want things she wasn't sure she was capable of holding on to, but the expression on Beatrice's face let Abby know that wouldn't be the right answer. Beatrice wasn't asking the question as Rose Hall's owner, but as a mother who wanted to know if her son had finally found himself. She was desperately hoping that Quinn had grown into the man she knew he was capable of being.

"He has been fantastic," Abby said, leaning forward slightly in an effort to make sure Beatrice knew just how sincere she was being. "He's worked harder than anyone else. He's found great solutions to huge problems. He's strengthened the estate's relationship with its suppliers. He's been incredible."

Beatrice turned, looking out of the window. Abby leant back, pretending not to notice the glistening in the other woman's eyes.

"To be honest with you," Abby said, "I feel a bit cheeky that you've still been paying me the full amount, given how much of my work Quinn has done over the last few months."

At that, Beatrice's head spun back around, her gaze fixing on Abby. "I know exactly how hard you have worked," she said. "And you have definitely earned every single penny, and more. Which is what I wanted to talk to you about."

Abby frowned, not sure where Beatrice was going now.

"I'm getting to the stage where I don't want my whole life to be wrapped up in this estate. I want to spend time with my granddaughter, and hopefully future grandchildren. I want to be able to visit my daughter whenever I please. Part of making that happen is getting more help here. I have spoken to the managers here and they cannot speak highly enough of you. As such, I'd like to offer you the events manager role on a permanent basis," Beatrice said.

Abby opened her mouth to reply, feeling slightly stunned, but Beatrice held her hand up.

"Don't answer now," Beatrice said. "Take some time to consider the offer. You'd be able to stay in your current room or move into one of the estate cottages if you'd prefer not to be in the main house. Or you could settle in Honeyford. I know a few of the younger members of staff travel in from the village."

"I, um…" Abby started, not sure what she was going to say. Given how much time she'd spent trying to avoid thinking about what she would do after this summer, she had never considered this possibility.

The only thing she could think now was that if she accepted, it could only be for the long term. It would be wrong to accept without being certain she could stick around.

"I appreciate you weren't expecting this, so please take some time," Beatrice said. "If you do decide to leave, we can work through a handover during the week after the ball as we'd originally planned."

"But —" Abby said, not sure how she was going to say this, but knowing she couldn't let Beatrice make this offer without knowing.

"I appreciate you haven't been out of the military for that long, so it will take you some time to decide what you want to do," Beatrice said, interrupting her and fixing Abby with a gaze so intense that she knew military officers who'd pay good money to be trained by this woman. "The last thing I will say on this subject before you come to me with your decision, is this…" Beatrice paused. "I would hope that a sensible woman such as yourself wouldn't let the status or otherwise of their relationship with a man determine their career."

Abby swallowed; well, that answered that question. Beatrice was very much aware of the fact she and Quinn were more than colleagues, and she was also seemingly aware that their relationship was complicated.

"But —" Abby said again, still not sure that she would accept. She didn't know what would be worse: working here without Quinn when he returned to his city life, or working here with him if he chose to stay, but not actually being with him when their relationship inevitably ended.

"I mean what I say," Beatrice said, her expression still serious. "No matter what, I hope you accept."

CHAPTER THIRTY-FIVE

"Thank you," Quinn said, smiling at his sister as she tucked her clothes back into place, his sated niece dozing quietly in her arms. The occasional snuffle made Quinn smile. "Who knew having a sister with her own clothing business would be so helpful? I just hope Abby likes it."

"Quinn," Cordelia said. "I have never had a customer buy an outfit for someone else with so much care."

"What if she doesn't like it, though?" he asked, shoving his hair back from his face.

"You know she likes dresses but has a lot of issues with their practicality. Your requirements were so specific, and so clearly perfect for the Abby that I've gotten to know over the last few days, that she is going to love it," Cordelia said. "I just wish you hadn't insisted on paying."

"I know you do," Quinn said, his mouth twisting at the memory of how hard Cordelia had argued with him on that point.

He knew charging her own brother made her feel awkward, but the dress was his gift to Abby, his attempt at showing her that he saw her, every part of her. That he heard her, and could be trusted to always hear her.

"What are you two bickering about?"

The familiar voice made Quinn turn. The sight of Abby dressed in her running gear made his lip curl into the smile that always felt more natural than the one he'd been using for years. She'd run almost every morning since he'd met her, but the evening runs were new. There was a small part of him that hoped this was being driven by a need to sort her own thoughts, that she wasn't finding the prospect of leaving Rose Hall as straightforward as she'd expected.

"Oh, you know, annoying little sisters," Quinn said.

"I'd say it's usually more the annoying older brother," Abby retorted, giving him a wink, before turning her gaze to Cordelia.

"I can't believe you're running in this heat," Cordelia said.

"I was hoping it would be a bit cooler by now," Abby smiled.

"It might help if you wore something without sleeves," Quinn said, holding her gaze with the challenge. Abby had his sister and mother's gift of being comfortable with who she was, but Quinn was determined that she would see that she didn't need to hide her scars, that she would accept that final part of herself.

Abby simply raised her eyebrows and gave him a smile that made him want to stand up, pull her against him, and forget that his sister was there.

"I'll see you in a bit," she said. Without waiting for a response she turned, heading away from him, her speed building until she reached the edge of the treeline and the pathway curved.

"She hasn't made a decision yet, then?" Cordelia asked, rocking Mia in her arms.

Quinn shook his head, keeping his attention on the footpath, his vision filled with the woman he loved even though she had disappeared from view.

"Have *you* made a decision yet?" Cordelia asked.

Quinn flinched. He wasn't surprised his sister had made the connection between his own indecision and Abby's, but he hadn't been prepared for her to call him on it. "A decision about what?" he asked, deciding it was better to play ignorant.

Lifting the jug, he topped up both of their glasses of water. He had learned lots about new mothers in the last few days, so he knew Cordelia needed to keep her fluids up while she was breastfeeding. It was easier to think about practical things than to deal with his feelings.

"You know what," Cordelia said, rolling her eyes.

"She hasn't asked," Quinn said, wishing he'd managed to stop the words from coming out in that whiney tone that reminded him of being a whole lot younger.

The sensible part of Quinn's brain knew that he didn't need to be asked, that heading Rose Hall was his for the taking. A small part of him wanted to be asked, though. His mother had made the offer plenty of times in the past, but he wanted to be asked again now that he'd proved it wouldn't be a request based solely on the luck of his birth. He hoped his mother now believed he was actually up to the job.

Quinn hadn't said anything to Cordelia about how much he wanted to stay at Rose Hall, because he knew the moment he did, he'd be backed into a corner. He might be able to say he'd changed his mind later on, that he'd decided it wasn't for him, but in doing so he would hurt Beatrice more than he'd ever be able to live with. It was better to wait.

"Mother isn't going to ask you again," Cordelia said. "This is your inheritance. You don't have to run it yourself, but you can't expect her to run it for you forever."

"It's hers at the moment," Quinn said, hiding behind an argument even he knew was weak. He was determined not to let Cordelia guess at his hopes for the future, not before he was absolutely certain he was ready to commit to them. However much he wanted to be here, he wanted to be with Abby more.

"Doesn't Mother deserve some time off before she dies?" Cordelia asked.

"Don't even talk about that," Quinn said firmly. "She's only just sixty."

"Yes, and you've seen just how much work this place takes," Cordelia said.

Quinn turned away from his sister, his frustration building. There was no way he could live with being the Beaumont who presided over the sale or, even worse, decline, of Rose Hall, and he didn't want to let the sheer hard work the place took drive his mother into an early grave like it had their father. His love for the place was growing. If he was honest, it had never gone away — he'd just supressed it for the last few years. He could see his life here, working his hardest to help Rose Hall thrive, but when he closed his eyes, his dreams of being here all included Abby at his side. As much as he loved the place, he wanted more from his life than obligation to an estate.

"Have you and Abby talked about this?" Cordelia said, adjusting her daughter in her arms.

Quinn smiled at the sight of his niece's face scrunching up as she was jostled. Shaking his head, his gaze travelled back to the trail Abby had taken into the woods. "I don't know how to," he said quietly. "Whenever I've tried, she's pulled back so far and so fast that I can't risk it again."

He couldn't look at Cordelia; he didn't know what he would see if he did, but he knew he wouldn't like it. His sister had never been scared of anything. She'd thrown herself at life with an energy and courage that Quinn had always envied. If Cordelia wanted something, she'd simply made it happen, her certainty barrelling her through without hesitation. Unfortunately, one summer of feeling competent wasn't going to erase the years of self-doubt that Quinn had been living with.

"Have you considered that it doesn't have to be all or nothing?" Cordelia said, finally breaking the silence.

Quinn turned to face his sister; what on earth was she talking about? With someone as incredible as Abby, only having part of her would be as painful as having none. He couldn't live with not knowing that she was as all in as he was.

Cordelia smiled at him, her expression full of understanding. "I don't mean Abby. I mean this place," she said, waving her free arm towards the building that towered over her. "You could be head of the estate, but that doesn't mean you have to be here full-time."

Concentrating on Cordelia's words, Quinn tried to work out what she meant, the building sounds of Mia's cries making it hard to focus.

Standing, he gestured for his sister to hand over his niece, and as he lifted Mia against his chest, he began to gently sway. As he smiled at the way the tiny bundle settled almost instantly, his heart swelled.

"It's a job like any other. Just because Mother takes on day-to-day duties and fills her time with the place doesn't mean you have to," Cordelia continued, stretching out and relaxing now her daughter was settled. "The team here are experienced and capable. You could just set the direction and check in from time to time."

Quinn's movements stopped as he absorbed his sister's words. His niece quickly made her feelings about that known and Quinn began to sway again. Perhaps Cordelia was right; other than the odd crisis, there were enough professionals here to run Rose Hall. Could he run Rose Hall and still be wherever Abby needed to be?

CHAPTER THIRTY-SIX

Stepping out of her bathroom, Abby tightened the towel wrapped around her head. Her attention was quickly drawn to the garment bag on her bed, which sat next to the suit she had laid out before going for a shower.

Moving to the bed, Abby lifted the small envelope that was positioned carefully on top of the bag. Recognising Quinn's handwriting, she frowned and ripped it open. Lifting a folded sheet of paper out, she read the message:

I hope this one is more to your taste, love Quinn x

Love. He hadn't said that word to her, but he'd written it. Was it simply habit, or did he mean it? At the possibility he meant it, her heart soared before seeming to drop like a lead weight. This would be so much easier if he didn't love her back, if he was just using her to pass the summer. Everything inside of her rebelled at that idea, but it didn't mean she was wrong.

Finally, curiosity overcame the maelstrom of emotions that were churning inside. She would have to give her decision to Beatrice tomorrow, and she wasn't sure if she could do it.

As she unzipped the garment bag, a silky khaki material was revealed. She smiled; she might be a civilian now, but years of military service meant that she loved the colour. Abby pushed at the edges until she could feel the hanger and lifted it out. The sleeveless dress had epaulets on the shoulders, featuring three gold chevrons, and a long hidden zip at the side. Placing it back on the bed, Abby studied it, before shrugging off her dressing gown.

Pulling the dress on, she realised that it had been designed so she could do it up herself. Once she had it fastened, she allowed herself to turn and face the freestanding mirror. It fit perfectly, the fabric moulding to her figure without clinging, before flaring at her waist. The full skirt reached the top of her feet, but was just the perfect length to be elegant, without hampering her movements. Skimming her hands down her ribs and along the flare, she realised something else. Pockets. The dress had pockets.

Her brain seemed to stutter; the fact that Quinn had been this thoughtful, that he'd listened to and remembered her preferences in such detail, almost took her breath away. Stepping backwards, she sank onto the bed, her movements making the garment bag slide onto the floor. As it fell, Abby caught a glimpse of more khaki.

Wondering what else could be in the bag, she bent, and pulled out a much smaller piece of fabric, and with it another envelope. Turning the material in her hands, she realised it was a shrug, the sleeves just long enough to reach her elbows. Opening the envelope, she scanned the words that were once again in Quinn's scrawling handwriting:

I hope you know you don't need to wear this, every inch of you is perfect, but it's here in case it helps you feel more comfortable.

Glancing at the top of her left arm, Abby realised that she hadn't even noticed the puckered scar tissue when she'd looked in the mirror. It was the first time she could remember since the ambush that she hadn't even registered that she was wearing something that had straps instead of sleeves. Quinn had done that for her. He was trying to nudge her towards a place where she didn't feel the need to hide them, but even now he wasn't forcing the issue. It was her choice.

He'd been extremely vocal about the fact she didn't need to hide her scars. He'd actually gone so far as to suggest she should be proud of them, because she should be proud of every part of who she was. Other people had said as much to her over the last few years — her family, her friends — but for the first time she actually felt it. Somewhere deep inside, a belligerent flame of defiance flickered to life; it seemed to be a challenge for people to look at her scars and for their face to twist up. Let them judge her for trying to save her colleagues, her friends. The sense of confidence felt like a sudden change, but Abby realised that it had crept up on her over the course of the summer, much like her love for Quinn. No matter how afraid she had been that she couldn't commit to anyone, her heart was entirely his, and Abby knew that it always would be.

After drying her hair, Abby twisted it up into her usual bun. She might be wearing a ballgown, but she was still working, and that meant she didn't want the hassle of dealing with her hair. As a compromise, she applied a little more make-up than usual. A glance at her watch let her know she needed to get downstairs, so she would be on hand to deal with the guests as they arrived.

As she walked into the hallway, she smiled at the sight of Quinn. Her stomach swooped as she took in his profile; he was pulling faces as he bounced his niece up and down in his arms. He was always attractive, but dressed in a dark evening suit with a khaki pocket square, which matched her dress, there was something slightly otherworldly about him.

Swallowing hard, she pushed thoughts of looming decisions to the back of her mind. For now, she was going to focus on ensuring the final event of the season went well, and she was going to enjoy herself. The future could wait for tomorrow.

"You look beautiful," Quinn said when she reached his side, and Abby smiled as he leaned towards her.

She took a step backwards, giving him a teasing smile. "That'll have to wait for later. We have work to do."

"Abby," Lisa said, appearing in the hallway, her expression panicked. "We need your help. One of the guests has managed to rip their dress down the back."

"Okay," Abby said, turning her attention to Lisa. "Lead the way."

"Wow," Lisa said. "That dress is amazing."

"Thank you." Abby glanced over her shoulder at Quinn. Unsurprisingly, there was a look of satisfaction on his face. Giving him a wink, she wondered if Quinn could see that she was entirely in love with him.

The first couple of hours of the ball passed in a whirl as Abby leapt from one crisis to another — stapling one dress together, sponging a spillage from another and then helping the serving staff when one guest became irate because they'd run out of smoked salmon blinis. Throughout the evening Abby's gaze kept searching for Quinn, a sense of warmth and belonging filling her whenever their eyes met. His frustrated smiles making her want to giggle as he seemed to be cornered by one person after another, all desperate for his attention.

"Could you follow me?" Lisa said, as the tempo of the music changed, and people started moving to the dancefloor. Abby's attention turned from where Quinn was chatting to a jowly man on the other side of the room and focused on Lisa.

Abby didn't bother asking what the problem was this time. After following Lisa through the corridors, she realised they were headed to Mrs Barclay's office.

"What —" Abby started to ask as she pushed the door open, the question dying on her lips as she took in the sight in front of her.

"Shut the door quickly," Mrs Barclay said, her tone one of mock seriousness.

"Yes, we don't want that lot to find us," Lisa said with a giggle.

Abby smiled, taking in the array of canapés spread across Mrs Barclay's desk and the bottle of champagne that was chilling in an ice bucket.

"We deserve a break," Mrs Barclay said, leaning back in her chair and popping a smoked salmon blini into her mouth.

"So, this is why we've run out," Abby laughed.

"Donna made these for the staff," Lisa said. "But we know you well enough to know you won't stop working long enough to eat anything yourself, so here we are."

"You did this for me?" Abby asked.

"We did," Lisa said, crossing the room and slipping her arm around Abby's waist and leading her to a chair. "We're officially on our break, so we figured you could be too."

"Thank you," Abby said, her voice cracking slightly as she tried to keep her emotions in check.

"So, what do you think of Mr Fetheringstone's suit?" Mrs Barclay asked, her eyebrows waggling up and down.

"Is he the man in the knitted suit?" Abby asked.

"Yes!" Lisa giggled. "He's very proud of it. He knitted it himself. I think he's worn it for the last three years."

"Well, knitting something so complicated is certainly impressive," Abby said, her lips twitching.

"It would be more impressive if he'd chosen a tighter knit. At least that way we wouldn't have to see his underpants peeking out through the pattern when he bends over," Mrs Barclay said, laughing hard.

"Oh God. I was trying to convince myself that was just the light," Abby said, joining in with the laughter.

Watching her colleagues and friends, Abby realised that she truly felt at home here. The idea of leaving seemed to pull at something inside of her. She wanted to stay. She wanted to keep on being a part of this amazing team. She'd missed the camaraderie of the army, and while this was different, it was just as good in its own way. This was what she'd been looking for. Could she do it? Could she remain here? As soon as the questions formed, they were followed by the realisation that it wasn't her decision to make.

Break long over, Abby realised that Lisa and Mrs Barclay had been right: if they hadn't secreted her away, she wouldn't have had a moment to eat, but at least things seemed to be settling down. The guests were busy dancing or drinking, or both. Beatrice was being twirled around the dancefloor by an old friend of her husband, and Quinn was walking across the ballroom towards Abby.

"Would you do me the honour of a dance?" he asked.

Abby nodded, wanting nothing more than to be in his arms.

Quinn slipped his hand into hers, and she let herself enjoy the moment as he led her to the dancefloor. As they found a space, the music changed, something slow and haunting and sensual playing. Almost without instruction, Abby found herself leaning against Quinn, enjoying the feeling of being in his arms again.

"I wish we could do this forever," Abby said, the words slipping out before she could stop them.

Quinn froze for a moment, before moving again. "We could," he said. "My mother has been pushing me to take over for longer than I care to remember."

Abby tensed in his arms. His first two words had made her believe, for a fleeting moment, that she could have everything she wanted, but then he had continued talking. It was clear his resentment at the obligation of Rose Hall hadn't entirely vanished, and in that moment, Abby knew she would never be the reason he stayed. She would never be the reason he didn't become the man he was capable of being. She would never add to the pressure he was under to take over here.

"You look so beautiful," he said, once more backing away from any discussion of the future. This time, though, she wasn't grateful. This time, she knew what she wanted, and the pain of realising that having a future together would mean they both had to be ready, that they both had to know what they wanted, seemed to suck all the air from her lungs. Focusing on keeping her movements smooth, she waited for her breathing to stabilise.

If she was sensible, she would pull out of his arms right now, but the idea that he would never hold her again made her want to be selfish. She would allow herself this final moment with Quinn, then she would face reality. She would step back and give him the space he needed, even though he didn't want it.

"The dress looks wonderful on you," Quinn said, his voice soft. His hand moved slightly on her lower back, sending a wave of longing through Abby. She took a deep breath. There was no point wishing for something that didn't exist because, whether she liked it or not, he needed to find out who he was, and that meant he didn't need her. She wouldn't stay at Rose Hall without him. She couldn't.

"Thank you for arranging it," she said, her words soft, wanting him to understand how much she appreciated the gesture.

"I'm glad you didn't wear the jacket," Quinn said, one hand gently touching her elbow before it slid up her arm, the contact barely perceptible as his fingers traced the path his lips had followed many times that summer. The warmth of his touch over the puckered skin of her scars made Abby wish for something she finally accepted she was ready for.

How had it come to this? She could finally see a future in one place, with one person, but she knew a relationship based on one person's needs wouldn't work. As much as Quinn deserved the space to decide his future for himself, she deserved a partner who knew their own mind. No matter how much Quinn had grown this summer, his future was still a mystery to him.

Abby blinked hard, attempting to rein her emotions back into place. She couldn't do this. She couldn't feel his arms around her, his fingers tracing her skin; she couldn't deal with sensations that were so familiar they filled her with a longing that could never be satisfied.

Taking another deep breath, she stepped backwards, using her arms to keep Quinn where he was. No matter how much she wanted him, she would give Quinn what he needed.

"Thank you for the dress," Abby said, her gaze fixed over his shoulder, her back as straight as if she'd been on parade. "I'd better get back to work."

"Abby," Quinn said, his tone pleading, his hand moving, resting on her arm as though to hold her in place.

Abby dropped her gaze to his hand, and he instantly let go. She felt as though her heart was going to break. That small gesture showed a level of respect that wasn't as common as it should be, and it also showed just how incredible Quinn could be. She wouldn't force that choice, though. With a small shake of her head, Abby turned, walking away from the future she'd dared to dream.

CHAPTER THIRTY-SEVEN

Standing at the door to Mrs Beaumont's drawing room the next morning, Abby took a deep breath. It was the first night she'd spent in her own room since that first night with Quinn, and it was also the worst night's sleep she'd endured in as long. Mrs Beaumont's words about not letting a man dictate her future swirled in her mind as she knocked.

"Abby," Mrs Beaumont said, the pleasure in her expression dropping as she took in Abby's rigid posture and carefully blank expression. She gestured for her to take a seat. "I'm not going to like your decision, am I?"

"I can't accept," Abby said, her response simple, knowing that if she made any effort to soften her decision, she wouldn't be able to hide her own turmoil.

"You seem happy here," Mrs Beaumont said, leaning back almost imperceptibly, her gaze searching Abby's face.

"I have been incredibly happy here," Abby said. No matter how she felt now, she had to be honest about that.

"Then why leave us?" Mrs Beaumont asked. For a brief moment, a flash of deeper concern crossed the older woman's face, but it vanished as she flicked at an invisible speck on the arm of her jacket.

"I haven't spent long in any one place for years," Abby said.

Mrs Beaumont studied her, as though seeing so much more than Abby was saying. Only her years of training kept Abby from squirming.

"It is none of my business, but I was hoping you would stay. I was hoping that your feelings for my son would keep you here, that they would keep you both here," Mrs Beaumont said, her words soft.

"Quinn has started to see himself for the man I know he is, the man we both know he is," Abby said, giving Mrs Beaumont a twisted smile. "But he still can't see his own future."

Mrs Beaumont looked away at that, and Abby's heart sank even further. Quinn's own mother knew the truth of Abby's words.

"I won't be some sort of prop for him," Abby said, knowing her words sounded cold, even before Mrs Beaumont's head swung back around and she glared at her. "He needs to make his own decisions. He needs the space to work out what he wants for himself, free of anyone else's influence."

"So, you are letting his indecision dictate your own choices," Mrs Beaumont said. The words were quiet, but Abby could feel the weight behind them.

"I am choosing to protect myself," Abby said, her own words equally quiet. "To protect him."

Mrs Beaumont let the silence build between them. It was a technique Abby knew well; she'd used it enough on her own squad over the years, but she finally realised she owed this woman the truth. Mrs Beaumont had been good to her, and Abby wanted her to understand that this choice wasn't about being weak.

"I won't survive being here without him," Abby said bluntly.

"He would stay with you?" Mrs Beaumont asked.

Abby shrugged. "I don't know."

"You're worried that if he stays, he'll resent you for it in the end," Mrs Beaumont said, and Abby's gaze swung up. "Don't be surprised. Why do you think I haven't forced his hand and made him come back before now?"

"You want him to choose to be here," Abby said, realising that she had more in common with Quinn's mother than she'd realised.

Mrs Beaumont nodded, seeming to age in front of Abby's eyes. For the first time, Abby noticed the creasing at the sides of her eyes, the lines on her neck, and the paleness of her complexion.

"I'm just as afraid he wouldn't choose to stay," Abby said, realising that she wanted to share her fears. Mrs Beaumont was probably the only person in the world who would understand Abby's position.

"Indeed," she said, holding her gaze sadly.

Finally back in the sanctuary of her room, Abby closed the door and leant against it. Her meeting with Mrs Beaumont had lasted less than twenty minutes, but it felt like the longest twenty minutes of her life. It wasn't as bad as the times she'd paced, waiting for news of the people she'd been responsible for, the times she'd waited to hear if they would survive their injuries, but it still hurt.

Abby would give herself this moment, she decided. Just this moment to deal with everything she was walking away from, and then she would pack and leave. She wouldn't live a life where she was anything less than everything to someone else. And unfortunately, Quinn didn't have enough faith in himself to be sure of what he wanted, not yet.

Her chest was so tight that she wondered if she was having a heart attack. Sliding down until she was sitting on the floor, she rubbed at her breastbone. Reaching up to her face, she realised that for the first time in as long as she could remember, she was crying. It was certainly the first time she had cried for herself. Her tears had always been reserved for those she had lost.

CHAPTER THIRTY-EIGHT

The next morning, the office remained occupied only by Quinn, and he felt his frown deepen. He shifted some papers, not registering anything on them, but unable to sit still. He hadn't been able to find Abby when the ball had ended last night, and she hadn't come to his room. He'd searched the house again but had faltered at her closed bedroom door. He was grateful that his mother and sister would be oblivious to the number of times he'd risen from his own bed, strode along the hallway determined to see Abby, and then frozen with his hand inches from her door.

She hadn't chosen to join him, and he wanted to respect that, but the implications terrified him. After a sleepless night he'd been here early, but it was almost nine-thirty and there was still no sign of her. He stood, deciding he couldn't keep ignoring this. He needed to lay his cards on the table, and then he had to hope like hell that he didn't lose her.

Pushing the door open, he headed up the stairs to the family quarters. His gaze instantly moved to Abby's door, but he had to do this right, and that meant speaking to his mother first.

"Enter," Beatrice's voice called when he knocked on the door.

He was surprised to find her sitting by the window, her body turned, as though she'd been staring out at the grounds. Beatrice was always in a flurry of activity; she never simply enjoyed the view. As she turned to face him, he took in the heavy shadows under her eyes, the wrinkles that seemed to have deepened overnight.

"Quinn," she said, her tone welcoming, even if her smile was forced.

"Are you okay?" he asked, crossing the space between them and crouching in front of her.

"I'm just tired," she said, her smile seeming even more brittle with her words.

Cordelia's words about their mother deserving to enjoy her next few years clanged through Quinn's head. The sight of his normally energetic mother so worn out made him even more certain he was doing the right thing. He lifted her small hands in his.

"I want to take over Rose Hall," he said, holding her gaze.

Beatrice frowned at him. "I'm not ill," she said, pulling her hands out of his. "I simply have jet lag and a new granddaughter who doesn't believe in sleep — and I've just been to a ball. Anyone would be tired."

"That's not why I want to take over," Quinn said, standing up and taking the seat opposite.

"Then why?" Beatrice asked, her tone challenging.

"I love it here," Quinn said, looking out of the window with a smile.

"You've refused for a very long time. What's changed?"

Quinn took in her frown. Part of him had expected her to be so delighted that she'd just agree and hand over the reins immediately, but he realised he was glad she wasn't doing that. She wanted him to prove he was ready, and her expression made it abundantly clear that she wasn't going to let him take control unless she was satisfied he was.

"I never wanted something that was just handed to me, because of who I am," Quinn said, waving his hand to keep her quiet as she opened her mouth to protest. "I didn't want to be the useless heir who would never have been given this responsibility if not for my last name."

"That would never have been the case," Beatrice protested.

"It would," Quinn said seriously. "You know my reputation, and you know it isn't entirely undeserved." He gave a rueful smile when she didn't argue. Pacing the room, he continued. "I wanted to be wanted for what I could do, for my abilities, not my name."

"And now?"

"This summer has shown me just what I'm capable of, and while I still have a lot to learn, I want to take my place in the incredible team here," he said, smiling.

"Because of Abby," Beatrice said. Something about her tone caught Quinn off guard.

"Partly," he said. "She helped me see what I'm capable of, but I finally feel like I know who I am." He laughed. "I appreciate that sounds a bit like I've been wandering around gazing at my navel and pondering my existence, but I don't mean it like that. Abby has helped me see who I am, but I had to do the work to see it, to accept it." He paused and walked back to the window, looking out for a moment before turning to his mother.

"You must not base who you are on someone else, though," Beatrice said, her frown deepening.

Quinn smiled, knowing exactly what she meant, and knowing that she was worrying needlessly. "I know who I am, and I have come to like that person. I'm excited to see what I can do with the help of the team here. But…" He paused for a moment. "I do need to be honest with you. How I do this, how I shape my role here, will be down to Abby."

Beatrice looked concerned, but Quinn knew that the next bit was something he had to share with Abby first. He owed her that much.

Finally back where he'd been so many times in the night, Quinn rapped on Abby's door, almost in time with his heartbeat. He wondered if he should knock louder, but before he could, the woman he'd been desperate to see swung the door open and stood in front of him.

"Can I come in?" Quinn asked, his voice wavering at the sight of her swollen eyes. The blotches on her face let him know that this steady, capable woman had been reduced to tears. Guilt that he could be the cause of her distress warred with the hope it gave him, because if she was this upset, perhaps she really did want to stay.

Abby nodded, before stepping back to allow him to enter. The sight of a half-packed bag on her bed made his heart sink. He couldn't be too late, he just couldn't.

CHAPTER THIRTY-NINE

Abby's heart sank at the sight of Quinn. If she'd thought having this conversation with Beatrice had been hard, she knew it would be even worse having it with Quinn. She'd hoped she'd be packed and gone before he realised she was leaving. She might be strong enough to do what she knew was right for him, what would eventually be right for her, but she wasn't brave enough to do it in person. Leaving a note was cowardly, but it was all she was capable of. Unfortunately, with Quinn in front of her, it looked as if that wouldn't be an option.

"You're leaving?" he said.

She simply nodded, her voice failing her.

Quinn closed his eyes, as though battling something. When he opened them, he continued to keep his gaze away from her. "Were you going to say goodbye?" he asked, his voice so quiet that she barely heard the words.

"I couldn't," Abby said, her voice cracking as she spoke, her eyes fixed on the worn carpet.

Quinn moved closer. "Don't leave."

Abby swallowed, not knowing how to find the words to explain.

"I love you," Quinn said, the words so raw that Abby's head swung up without any instruction from her brain and she gasped.

The intensity of Quinn's gaze took her breath away. There was no doubting that he believed it, but that didn't change the fact he needed to work out what he wanted for himself before he'd truly be capable of loving anyone properly. It didn't change the fact that Abby knew only having part of him would eat away at her.

"You need to discover your own path before you can really mean those words," she said.

"I know my path," Quinn said. "I know it's with you, wherever you are."

Abby hadn't wanted to have to say this to him, but it was clear that Quinn wasn't going to accept anything less than the full truth. "I deserve more than someone who doesn't know what they want out of life. I deserve someone who accepts themselves, because that's the only way they can truly love me the way I should be loved. The way everyone deserves to be loved." Abby took a step backwards and wrapped her arms around her middle, needing a barrier.

"Do you love me?" Quinn asked, his body shifting, as though he was going to close the distance she had just created, before he stopped himself.

Abby shrugged. "Does it matter?" she asked.

"I've just been to see my mother," Quinn said, his head tilting as he spoke.

Abby's already pounding heart seemed to beat faster, her mind scanning the conversation she'd had with Beatrice. Had she shared their discussion with Quinn? Had Abby admitted that she loved Quinn?

"I have told her I want to take over as head of Rose Hall," he said. "After years of trying to persuade me to come home and do it, you wouldn't believe how hard I had to work to convince her to agree."

Abby met his gaze, her lips curling into a compressed smile. "You will be amazing," she said. "Rose Hall are lucky to have you."

"Perhaps," Quinn said with a shrug. "I suspect I'm luckier to have them." This time he did move, taking a single step closer to Abby. "But you're missing the important thing. I do know who I am, and I may have a lot to learn, but this summer has shown me exactly who I want to be. It's taught me that I'm capable of becoming that man."

Abby's smile grew at that; she wanted that for him. The first day she'd seen Quinn at Rose Hall, she'd seen the façade of confidence that he showed the world. She wanted that to be real.

"I also know that I love you." Quinn took another step closer to her. "Do you love me?" he asked again, closing the final distance between them.

Abby felt her body sway. "What if it's not enough?" she said, closing her eyes to avoid having to meet his unwavering gaze as she evaded his question.

"Abby, we can make it work," Quinn said, his fingers stroking her. "I know you are used to moving around, I know you are afraid that you won't be able to stay in one place, but we have options. I can be responsible for this place without being here all the time."

Abby's eyes flicked open. She was surprised that he'd understood her fears, but also that he didn't know she wasn't afraid of that anymore. She had been so worried about her own ability to stay here, to stay with him. The last few days had caused those fears to fade, the shift inside of her so monumental that she couldn't believe it wasn't obvious to everyone who looked at her.

"You've thought this through," she said, as her mind tried to process what Quinn was saying.

"Abby, for the first time in my life, I know what I want. I know what I want my future to look like, and I will do whatever it takes to make that happen."

Abby took a deep breath and closed her eyes again. Quinn wasn't just coming to her with some half-baked declaration of love. He was coming to her as someone taking ownership of his own life, as someone who had figured out his place in the world. Quinn was opening his heart and being vulnerable, but as the man she had known he was capable of being.

Opening her eyes, Abby held Quinn's gaze firmly in her own. "I love you," she said.

At her words, his arm shot around her waist and pulled her to him. The sensation of his chest pressed against her own filled Abby with warmth, and she slipped her arms around his neck, dragging his head down until his lips met hers.

"Thank God," Quinn said, the words muttered against her mouth as his hands pulled at her clothing, as though afraid she'd vanish if he didn't touch every inch of her skin.

"You were just worried you'd have to find a new events manager," Abby said with a giggle.

"Damn it," he said, the whispered words creating goosebumps as they travelled down her neck. "We need to find a way to make sure you're not as busy as you have been this year."

Abby pulled back and gave Quinn a questioning look.

"I'm going to want you to myself a lot more in the future," he said seriously.

"I'm definitely not going to argue about that," Abby said, pulling his lips back to hers, grateful that she'd found somewhere, someone, who made her want to stay.

A NOTE TO THE READER

Dear Reader,

Thank you so much for reading *Summer at Rose Hall*. Reviews by readers are incredibly important to authors' success these days, so if you enjoyed the novel and would consider taking the time to leave a review, your efforts would be hugely appreciated. Reviews can be left in many places, but you can access **Amazon** and **Goodreads** here.

I love hearing from readers, and would be delighted if you connected with me through my **Facebook page** via **Twitter** or through my **website**.

Here's to escaping into the pages of more heart-warming lives, and loves, together.

Tanya Jean

www.tanyajeanrussell.com

Sapere Books is an exciting new publisher of brilliant fiction and popular history.

To find out more about our latest releases and our monthly bargain books visit our website:
saperebooks.com